INSECTS
AND
SPIDERS
STICKER-PEDIA

Silver Dolphin

San Diego, California

SilverDolphin

Silver Dolphin Books

An imprint of the Advantage Publishers Group
5880 Oberlin Drive, San Diego, CA 92121-4794
www.silverdolphinbooks.com

Author: Jinny Johnson

Copyright © Marshall Editions, 2005

A Marshall Edition
Conceived, edited, and designed by Marshall Editions
The Old Brewery, 6 Blundell Street, London N7 9BH, U.K.
www.quarto.com

ISBN-13: 978-1-59223-557-5
ISBN-10: 1-59223-557-3

1 2 3 4 5 10 09 08 07 06

Originated in Singapore by Universal Graphics
Printed and bound in China by CT Printing
Publisher: Richard Green
Commissioning editor: Claudia Martin
Art direction: Ivo Marloh
Editor: Sharon Hynes
Design and editorial: Hart McLeod

The access code for your CD-ROM is:

INSECT

Contents

How to use this book   6

The world of insects and spiders   8

Story Pages

What is an insect?   10

What is an arachnid?   12

Insect senses   14

Legs and movement   16

Wings and flight   18

Bugs, lice, fleas, and beetles   20

Creature Pages   22

Story Pages

Feeding   26

Creature Pages   28

Play Pages

Rain forest   30

Creature Pages   32

Story Pages

Stag beetles   36

Grasshoppers, cockroaches, and relatives   38

Creature Pages   40

Story Pages

Metamorphosis   42

Creature Pages   44

Play Pages

Backyard   46

Creature Pages   48

Story Pages

Eggs and egg laying   52

Dragonflies, mantids, and relatives   54

Creature Pages   56

Story Pages

Self-defense   58

Play Pages

Pond   60

Creature Pages   62

Story Pages

Finding a mate   64

Flies, moths, and butterflies · 66

Creature Pages · 68
Story Pages
  Mosquitoes · 72
Play Pages
  Woodland · 74
Creature Pages · 76
Story Pages
  Sphinx moths · 78
Creature Pages · 80
Story Pages
  Camouflage, mimicry, and warnings · 82

Bees, wasps, ants, and termites · 84

Story Pages
  Social insects · 86
Creature Pages · 88
Story Pages
  Honeybees · 90
Creature Pages · 92
Play Pages
  Meadow · 94
Creature Pages · 96

Spiders, scorpions, slugs, and snails · 100

Story Pages
  Hunters · 102
Creature Pages · 104
Story Pages
  Trap setters · 110
Creature Pages · 112
Play Pages
  Desert · 114
Story Pages
  Young arachnids and insects · 116
Creature Pages · 118
Story Pages
  Creatures that glow · 120

Glossary · 122
List of creatures · 124
Acknowledgments · 128

STICKER SHEETS · 129
Animal Pages Stickers
  Insects · 129
  Arachnids · 147
Play Pages Stickers · 152

How to use this book

This Sticker-pedia has seven parts. In the first section, we introduce you to the world of insects and spiders. The second part is about bugs, lice, fleas, and beetles. The third looks at grasshoppers, cockroaches, and their relatives. The fourth section covers dragonflies, mantids, and their relatives. The fifth part is about flies, moths, and butterflies. The sixth is bees, wasps, ants, and termites. And then the last section is all about spiders, scorpions, slugs, and snails.

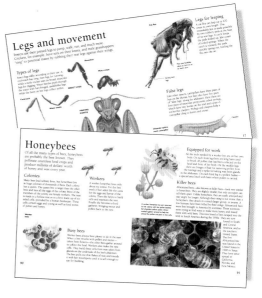

On the Story Pages, you can learn some interesting facts, such as how a scorpion kills its prey or how a lichen spider avoids being eaten.

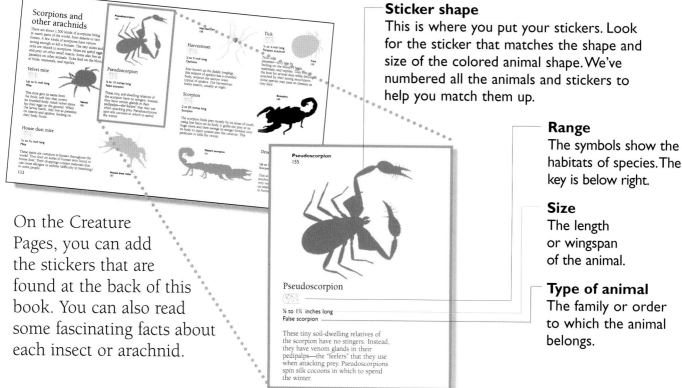

On the Creature Pages, you can add the stickers that are found at the back of this book. You can also read some fascinating facts about each insect or arachnid.

Sticker shape
This is where you put your stickers. Look for the sticker that matches the shape and size of the colored animal shape. We've numbered all the animals and stickers to help you match them up.

Range
The symbols show the habitats of species. The key is below right.

Size
The length or wingspan of the animal.

Type of animal
The family or order to which the animal belongs.

You can have even more sticker fun with the Play Pages. Try arranging your stickers in the different landscapes and water scenes.

Meadow play page

You can find the stickers of insects that live near flowers on pages 158–159. Stick them on this page to create your own meadow scene.

You'll find all your stickers at the back of the book. The stickers for the Creature Pages are on pages 129–151. The stickers for the Play Pages are on pages 152–160. Start sticking!

Key to habitat symbols

Worldwide	Temperate	Tropical

The world of insects and spiders

Insects outnumber every other creature on Earth. There are about one and a half million known animal species in the world, and about one million of those species are insects.

Arachnids, like insects, are found all over the world in every kind of habitat. There are at least 75,000 species of arachnids, of which spiders are the biggest group. Unlike insects, arachnids do not have wings or antennae. They have eight legs and their bodies are divided into two parts.

Insects and spiders are invertebrates, which means they have no backbones. Also in this book are creatures such as worms, snails, and centipedes, which are also invertebrates.

A gleaming mint leaf beetle settles on a mint leaf—its main food plant. Leaf beetles feed on the leaves and flowers of different plants and their larvae may attack the plant's roots. Many leaf beetles are serious pests to farmers' crops.

Garden snail

What is an insect?

Arthropods are the largest group of invertebrates. They have a hard external skeleton, called an exoskeleton, which protects the soft body within. An insect is an arthropod with six legs and a body arranged into three parts: head, thorax, and abdomen.

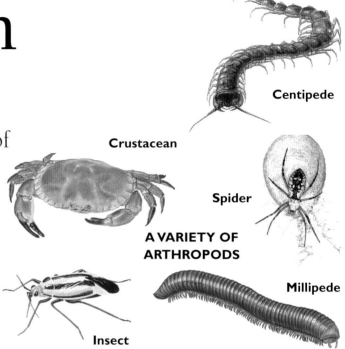

Centipede

Crustacean

Spider

A VARIETY OF ARTHROPODS

Millipede

Insect

An insect's body

An insect's thorax has three pairs of legs and, usually, two pairs of wings. (Insects are the only invertebrates that can fly.) The abdomen contains the heart, digestive system, and sexual organs. The head carries the eyes and antennae, as well as mouthparts, which vary in shape according to the insect's diet. Spongy or tubelike mouthparts mop or suck up food, while strong jaws chop up prey.

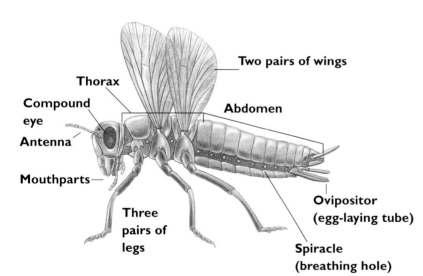

Two pairs of wings

Thorax

Compound eye

Antenna

Abdomen

Mouthparts

Three pairs of legs

Ovipositor (egg-laying tube)

Spiracle (breathing hole)

DIFFERENT TYPES OF MOUTHPARTS

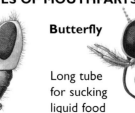

Housefly

Spongy mouthparts for mopping up liquid food

Butterfly

Long tube for sucking liquid food

Beetle

Strong jaws for cutting and piercing prey

Mosquito

Needlelike tube for sucking up food

Prehistoric bugs

The first bugs appeared over 300 million years ago. They were the first animals to fly. Most of these early species are now extinct, but fossils show that some were similar to the cockroaches and dragonflies of today. Some prehistoric insects were fossilized after getting trapped in muddy sediment, which later turned to rock. Others got stuck in resin oozing from tree trunks, which hardened to form amber.

A fly fossilized in amber about 250 million years ago

Molting

A caterpillar sheds its skin.

In order to grow to adult size, a young insect must molt—shed its hard exoskeleton—several times during its life. A new skeleton forms beneath the old one, and when it is ready to molt, the insect splits the old skeleton and wriggles out. Some young insects, such as caterpillars, have soft exoskeletons. They, too, molt several times before they grow a hard exoskeleton as an adult.

Pollination

To produce seeds, a flower must receive tiny pollen grains from another flower. As insects such as bees and butterflies feed on the pollen and nectar (a sugary liquid produced by flowers), pollen sticks to their bodies and is spread between flowers.

Pollen grains stick to bee's hair.

Bee sucks nectar from flower.

Bee stores pollen in leg sacs.

Other invertebrates

Earthworm

Slug

Snail

Many nonarthropod invertebrates live in the sea, including octopuses, squid, starfish, sponges, corals, and jellyfish. Others, such as snails, slugs, and earthworms, live on land. Slugs and snails make a slimy mucus that helps to keep their bodies from drying out and allows them to move more easily. Earthworms spend their lives burrowing through dirt.

What is an arachnid?

Arachnids—such as spiders, scorpions, and mites—are arthropods that have four pairs of walking legs. There are at least 70,000 different arachnid species, most of which live on land.

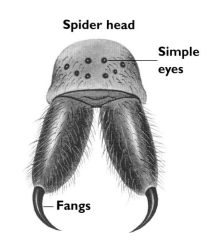

Spider head

Simple eyes

Fangs

Arachnid anatomy

Unlike insects, arachnids do not have a separate head. Instead, their head and thorax form one part, called the cephalothorax. This is linked to the abdomen by a narrow waist. At the front of the head are the jaws and mouth. Many arachnids have venom glands and give poisonous bites or stings. The pedipalps are sensory organs, which the males also use in mating or for grasping prey.

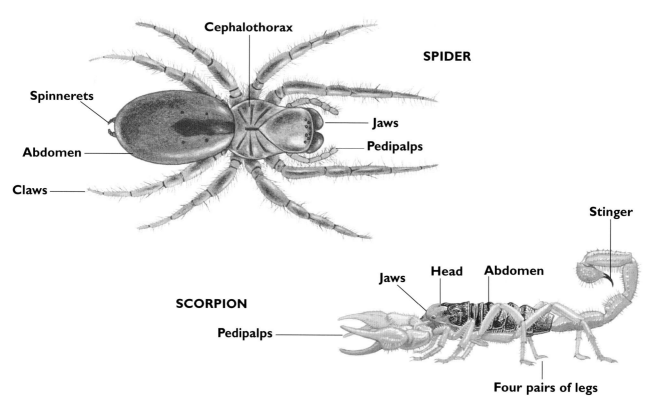

Cephalothorax

SPIDER

Spinnerets

Jaws

Abdomen

Pedipalps

Claws

Stinger

Jaws   **Head**   **Abdomen**

SCORPION

Pedipalps

Four pairs of legs

Building a web

While all spiders spin silk, not all use it to trap prey. Some spiders, such as orb weavers, build silken traps called webs. The silk is produced by glands at the end of the spider's abdomen. It is then released through nozzles, or spinnerets. This special silk hardens into a tough thread. The spider then weaves a framework of this silk, which it attaches to nearby plants or other supports. It then adds a spiral of a different, sticky silk to trap the prey.

Web of an orb weaver

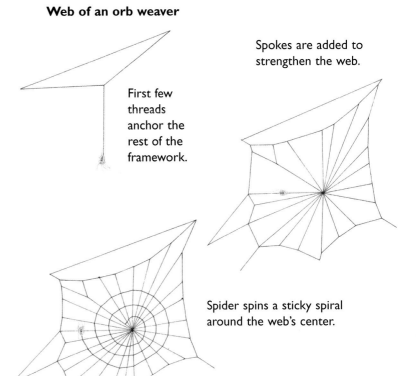

First few threads anchor the rest of the framework.

Spokes are added to strengthen the web.

Spider spins a sticky spiral around the web's center.

Spider spinnerets

Waiting on the web

After building its web, a spider waits at the center or hides close by. A signal thread allows the spider to feel vibrations caused by struggling prey caught on the web's sticky parts. The spider rushes over, bites the prey, and wraps it in silk to keep it from getting away. The prey can then be eaten at leisure.

13

Insect senses

Insects have antennae and tiny sense hairs that detect smells, tastes, vibrations, and sounds. Most insects have eyes, but sight is less important to them than it is to many other animals, including humans.

Wasp head

A wasp has a pair of large compound eyes that stretch down its cheeks and give it a wide field of view. It also has three simple eyes on the top of its head. The antennae register smells, while tiny sensory hairs detect sounds.

Antennae detect scents in the air.

Hairs on head feel vibrations caused by sound and movement.

Compound eyes are made up of many tiny lenses. They can detect the slightest movement.

Small, simple eyes detect light and darkness.

Talking by touch

Like many bugs, ants communicate with chemical signals. By touching antennae, they can send messages, alerting each other to danger or the location of food.

Avoiding bats

Bats catch insects by sending out high-pitched noises. These sounds bounce off nearby objects, alerting bats to the position of their prey. Moths have "ears" on their abdomen that can detect these sound-pulses. When a bat swoops in for the kill, a moth escapes by folding up its wings and dropping to the ground.

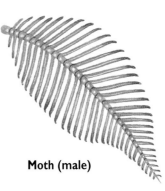

Mosquito (female)

Types of antennae

Antennae help an insect learn more about its surroundings. They are sensitive to touch and vibration, and also to airborne scents. Some antennae have many side branches so that there are more sensory cells and hairs. Arachnids have no antennae, but rely mostly on the sensory hairs on their bodies.

Cockchafer

Moth (male)

Legs and movement

Insects use their jointed legs to jump, walk, run, and much more. Crickets, for example, have ears on their knees, and male grasshoppers "sing" to potential mates by rubbing their rear legs against their wings.

Types of legs

Insect legs differ according to their use. A cockroach has long, lean legs for running, while a mole cricket uses its broad, muscular legs for digging. Water beetles push through the water with hair-fringed, paddlelike legs, while the hairs on bee legs collect pollen.

Honeybee

Mole cricket

INSECT LEGS

Cockroach

Water beetle

PRAYING MANTIS

Legs for grasping

Many insects have grasping legs, which they use to hold on to the opposite sex when mating, to fight off rivals, or to grip prey while feeding. A praying mantis's forelegs have strong muscles that allow it to clamp firmly around struggling prey while it is being eaten.

Sharp spines for gripping prey

16

Cat flea

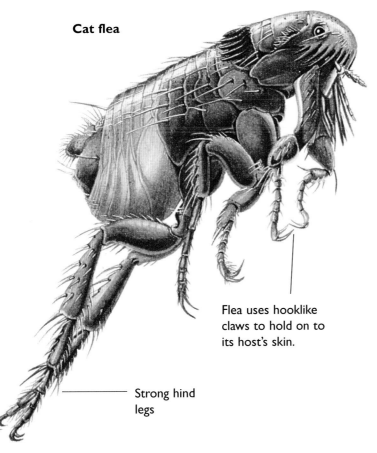

Legs for leaping

A cat flea can leap up to 200 times its own length. This remarkable feat is made possible by two rubbery pads at the base of its rear legs. A catch keeps the pads folded up, like a pair of coiled springs. When the catch is released, the pads quickly spring out, hurling the flea into the air.

Flea uses hooklike claws to hold on to its host's skin.

Strong hind legs

False legs

Like other insects, caterpillars have three pairs of legs on the thorax, but they also have five pairs of "false legs" along the abdomen. Here there are four pairs of muscular projections called prolegs, which have tiny hooks on the end and a pair of suckerlike claspers. Prolegs and claspers help a caterpillar cling to leaves and stems.

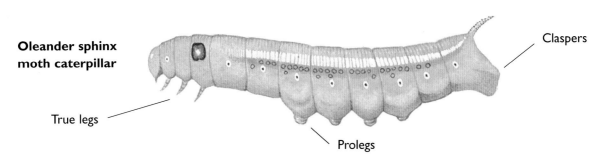

Oleander sphinx moth caterpillar

Claspers

True legs

Prolegs

17

Wings and flight

Arachnids cannot fly, but insects can, enabling them to escape from predators and travel far in search of food or a mate. Most insects have two pairs of wings.

The wing cases move forward and spread apart for flight.

Ladybug

Wing cases

The forewings of beetles, such as ladybugs, have evolved into hard, protective wing cases. For flying, beetles only use their hind wings, which are kept folded up beneath the wing cases until it is time for takeoff.

Large, transparent wings enable a ladybug to fly at fast speeds.

White-lined sphinx moth

Moth and butterfly wings

The scaly forewings and hind wings of moths and butterflies are linked so that they flap together. The whirring wings of sphinx moths beat so fast that the moths can hover while they feed on flower nectar.

Aerial stunts

A dragonfly flaps its four wings at the same time for fast, level flight. But by flapping the forewings and hind wings at different times, they can perform amazing acrobatics such as changing direction quickly, hovering, stopping in midflight, and even flying backward.

The wings are strengthened by a network of veins.

Darner dragonfly

Muscles in the thorax pull the wings up and down.

Fly halteres

In flies, the hind wings have developed into a pair of clublike structures called halteres. These flap up and down in opposition to the forewings, helping the fly to balance and change direction as it moves through the air. The halteres send information to the fly's brain so that it can avoid flying into objects.

Halteres stick out from the fly's thorax.

19

Bugs, lice, fleas, and beetles

Although the term "bug" is used for insects in general, it can also describe a particular group of insects. This includes a wide variety of species, including assassin bugs, stinkbugs, water boatmen, cicadas, and aphids.

Bugs, lice, fleas, and beetles are some of the most numerous of all insects. Bugs feed on a wide range of foods, from plant juices to human blood. Lice and fleas live as parasites, feeding on the blood, skin, feathers, and hair of other animals. Beetles form the largest group of insects and account for about 40 percent of known insect species. One of the reasons for their success is that they can survive on almost any type of food.

Ladybugs gather in large numbers in readiness for hibernation during the cold winter months.

Cat flea

21

Bugs, lice, and fleas

True bugs are one particular large group of insects. Most live on land, but some live in water. They all have beaklike mouthparts, with which they can pierce the body of a plant or animal and suck the fluids within. Lice are parasites that live on animals—including human beings—and suck their blood. Fleas are also parasites and are able to jump onto their hosts.

Cicada
1

Treehopper

¼ to ½ inch long
True bug

Many of these little bugs have strangely shaped body parts on their thorax that look like the sharp thorns of plants. They feed mostly on sap from trees and other plants.

Treehopper
2

Cicada

Up to 2 inches long
True bug

Cicadas are famous for their shrill, almost constant singing or chirruping. The male makes this sound by vibrating the drumlike organs, or tymbals, on its abdomen.

Aphid

Up to ⅜ inch long
True bug

These small, soft-bodied insects feed on sap from the leaves and stems of plants. This can damage plants. They reproduce very quickly, but many are destroyed by insects such as ladybugs and parasitic wasps.

Aphid
3

Stinkbug
4

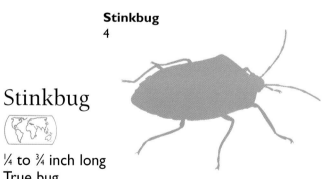

Stinkbug

¼ to ¾ inch long
True bug

Stinkbugs squirt a foul-smelling liquid at any creature that tries to attack them. The stinkbug uses its beaklike snout for piercing the surface of a plant or animal to get at the sap or body juices.

Plant bug

⅛ to ¾ inch long
True bug

The biggest group of true bugs, plant bugs live in every kind of habitat. Most feed on leaves, seeds, and fruit, and some are serious pests to farmers, as they feed on human food crops such as alfalfa.

Plant bug
5

Bedbug

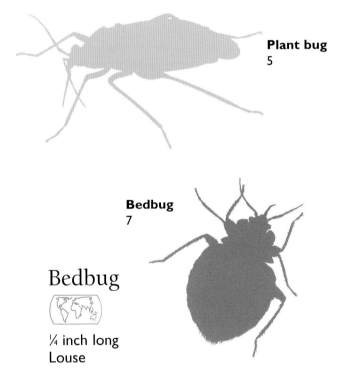

Bedbug
7

⅛ inch long
Louse

Bedbugs usually stay hidden during the day, then come out at night to feed on the blood of birds and mammals. Their flattened bodies make it easy for them to hide in crevices—they do not live on the bodies of their hosts. They often infest beds and mattresses, which explains their name.

Head louse

1/16 to ⅛ inch long
Louse

The head louse is a sucking louse that lives on human heads, feeding on blood. It holds on to hairs with its strong legs and claws, and glues its small eggs to the hairs of its host.

Head louse
6

Ambush bug

¼ to ½ inch long
True bug

The ambush bug lies in wait for prey and pounces when it comes near. Once it has attacked and killed an insect, it feeds on its body liquids.

Ambush bug
8

Spittlebug

⅛ to ½ inch long
True bug

Spittlebugs, also known as froghoppers, hop about on plants as they feed. When the larvae hatch, they cover themselves with a frothy substance like saliva, which protects them and helps them hide.

Assassin bug

½ to 2 inches long
True bug

Fierce-looking assassin bugs attack and kill other insects. When the bug has grasped its prey, it injects some saliva, which paralyzes its victim. The bug then sucks up the prey's body juices.

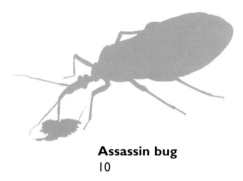

Assassin bug
10

Chigoe flea
11

Chigoe flea

⅛ to ¼ inch long
Flea

Like other fleas, chigoes live on the blood of humans and other animals. The flea causes a reaction in the host that makes the skin of the victim grow around the insect, forming a safe place for the female to lay her eggs.

Cat flea

Up to ¼ inch long
Flea

The cat flea can jump up to 200 times its own length. Spiny "combs" on the flea's head help to anchor it in the cat's fur. The flea also uses its hooklike claws to hold on to a cat's skin.

Cat flea
12

Feather louse

⅟₁₆ inch long
Louse

Feather lice live on a wide range of birds. They have two claws on each leg, which they use to cling to the bird's feathers. They feed on the feathers by biting off pieces with their strong jaws.

Feather louse
13

Bark louse

⅟₁₆ to ¼ inch long
Psocid

Bark lice are not lice at all but small insects called psocids. Most live outdoors on or under the bark of trees and bushes, and feed on lichen and algae. Others live in houses, and are often called booklice because they feed on mold, such as is found on old books.

Bark louse
14

Human flea

Up to ⅛ inch long
Flea

These fleas live in human dwellings—under furniture, in carpets, or in any place from which they can easily jump onto people to feed on their blood.

Human flea
15

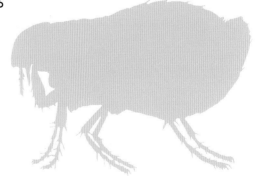

Feeding

Some insects feed on plants, while others get nourishment by sucking up liquids through strawlike tubes. Many insects are carnivores, or meat eaters, feeding on rotting meat or live prey.

Blowfly

Food liquidizers

Although many flies feed on solid food, they first have to turn it into liquid. To do this, they deposit saliva on the food to partially dissolve it. They mop up the resulting mushy liquid with a spongy pad on the end of their mouthparts.

Forelegs have taste buds.

Spongy pad absorbs the liquid.

Hummingbird sphinx moth

Tube probes deep into the flower.

Nectar drinkers

The feeding tube, or proboscis, of a butterfly or moth coils up under its head. When a moth or butterfly needs to feed, it uncoils the tube, dips it into a flower, and sucks up the sugary nectar, just as you would drink through a straw.

26

Bloodsuckers

Some insects feed on blood, which is rich in nutrients. A mosquito pierces an animal's skin with a needlelike tube and then sucks up the blood. It pumps saliva into the wound to keep the blood from clotting, so the victim's blood does not thicken and stop flowing. Only females bite animals—male mosquitoes feed on nectar.

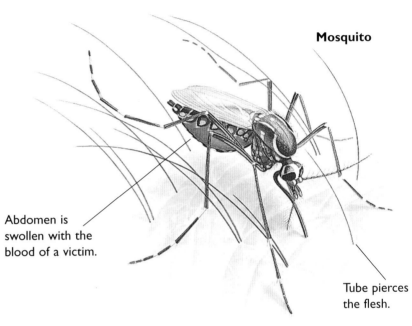

Mosquito

Abdomen is swollen with the blood of a victim.

Tube pierces the flesh.

Leaf chewers

A caterpillar has powerful jaws with overlapping teeth to chew up plant material. In some caterpillars, the jaws have developed into flat plates for grinding up tough leaves. When a caterpillar changes into an adult butterfly or moth, its mouthparts re-form as a long proboscis.

Water bugs

Some water bugs barely get wet—their feet are covered with waterproof hairs and they are so light they can run over the water without breaking the surface. Others live and hunt beneath the surface. Of these, some come to the surface to breathe from time to time. Some, such as water scorpions, have long breathing tubes at the end of their body. Others swim inside a single bubble of air that surrounds the body.

Water scorpion

Up to 4 inches long
True bug

This bug moves slowly through the water searching for prey, which it seizes with its powerful front legs. It has beaklike mouthparts and can give humans a painful bite.

Water scorpion
17

Water stick insect

Up to 2 inches long
Aquatic bug

This long, slender bug is a type of water scorpion, with a long breathing tube at the end of its thin body. Holding one end of this tube at the water's surface, it hangs with its head down, waiting for passing prey in the water.

Backswimmer

⅛ to ½ inch long
True bug

As their name suggests, backswimmers swim upside down. They move fast, using their back legs as oars. They hunt other insects and small creatures such as tadpoles, seizing their prey with their front legs and stabbing it with their beaks.

Backswimmer
16

Water stick insect
18

Water measurer

Up to 1 inch long
Aquatic bug

The water measurer walks on water plants or even across the surface of the water. It often spears food below the surface with its long, slender head.

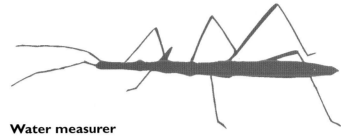

Water measurer
19

Water boatman
20

Water boatman

Up to ½ inch long
Aquatic bug

Unlike other water bugs, most water boatmen do not hunt animals but feed on tiny plants and algae. They collect their food with their front legs and use the middle and back legs for swimming.

Giant water bug

Up to 2½ inches long
True bug

Giant water bugs are the largest of the true bugs. They are strong swimmers that paddle with their back and middle legs and use their powerful front legs for catching prey.

Giant water bug
21

Rain forest play page

You can find the stickers of insects and spiders that live in tropical rain forests on pages 152–153. Stick them here to create your own rain forest scene.

Beetles

More than a quarter of a million species of beetles are known—and there are certainly many more yet to be discovered. They live in almost every type of habitat, from polar lands to rain forests, and feed on almost every type of food with their strong mouthparts. Beetles usually have two pairs of wings—the front pair is thick and hard and acts as a cover for the more delicate back wings.

Rove beetle
23

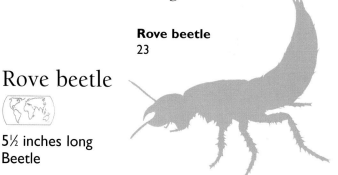

Rove beetle

5½ inches long
Beetle

This beetle has a long body and short wing cases. When it is disturbed, it raises the back end of its body, as a scorpion does. Unlike a scorpion, it does not sting—it bites. Adult rove beetles and their larvae both prey on insects and other small creatures such as worms.

Whirligig beetle

⅛ to ⅝ inch long
Aquatic beetle

Glossy whirligig beetles swim on the surface of ponds and streams, feeding on insects that fall into the water. Their eyes are divided into two parts so that they can see above and below the water's surface at the same time.

Goliath beetle
22

Goliath beetle

¾ to 5 inches long
Scarab beetle

The Goliath beetle, found in Africa, is one of the largest and heaviest of all insects. The males are the giants; the females are smaller and less brightly patterned. These beetles clamber into trees in search of sap and soft fruit to eat.

Tiger beetle

¼ to 1 inch long
Beetle

The colorful tiger beetle has long legs and is a fast runner. It is a fierce, active hunter. The female beetle lays its eggs in the sand. When the larvae hatch, they dig burrows, where they wait to grab passing prey.

Tiger beetle
24

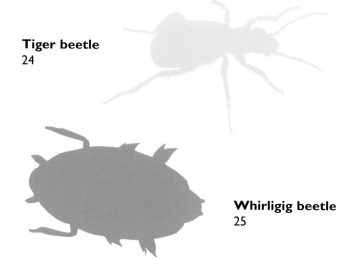

Whirligig beetle
25

Diving beetle

1/16 to 1/2 inch long
Aquatic beetle

Diving beetles live in ponds and lakes. They swim by moving their paddle-shaped back legs together, like oars. When they dive, the beetles can stay underwater for a long time, breathing air trapped under their wing cases.

Diving beetle
26

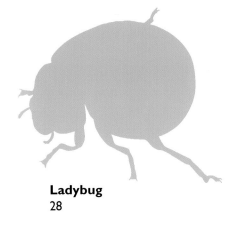

Scarab beetle

4/5 to 7 inches long
Scarab beetle

Scarabs are dung beetles. They roll animal dung into balls, bury the balls, and eat them at leisure. After mating, the female lays an egg in the center of a dung ball. The dung is the food for the newly hatched larva.

Scarab beetle
27

Ladybug

Up to 3/8 inch long
Winged beetle

Ladybugs help farmers and gardeners by feeding on aphids, which are pests that suck the juices of plants. The ladybug's bright colors warn its enemies that it tastes unpleasant and may be poisonous.

Ladybug
28

Firefly

Up to 1 inch long
Winged beetle

Fireflies, also known as lightning bugs, send out pulses of yellowish-green light from a special area at the end of their body. Each species flashes in a special pattern to attract mates of the same species. Larvae and wingless females are called glowworms.

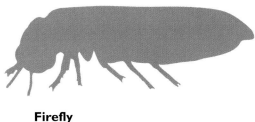

Firefly
29

Carrion beetle

Up to 1½ inches long
Beetle

Carrion beetles feed on dead animals, such as mice and birds. Some will lay eggs on a dead creature so that their young have a ready supply of food when they hatch. They are also called undertaker beetles.

Carrion beetle
30

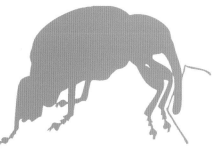

Jewel beetle
31

Jewel beetle

¾ to 2½ inches long
Scarab beetle

With their gleaming metallic colors, jewel beetles deserve their name. The larvae bore into dead or living wood as they eat and can cause a great deal of damage.

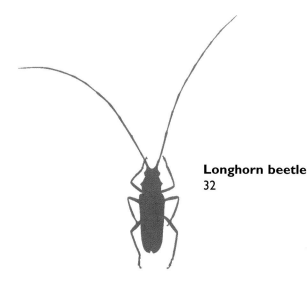

Longhorn beetle
32

Boll weevil
33

Longhorn beetle

7 inches long, including antennae
Beetle

This beetle has extremely long antennae—up to three times the length of its body. The male stands guard while the female lays her eggs in the crevices of living trees or logs.

Boll weevil

1/16 to 1½ inches long
Weevil

This insect belongs to the weevil family, all of which eat plants and can cause serious damage. The boll weevil uses its long snout to bore into the buds and seedpods, or bolls, of cotton plants.

Darkling beetle

½ to 1¾ inches long
Beetle

Common in dry areas, where they lurk under stones, darkling beetles scurry out at night to feed. They are scavengers, searching through garbage for food, and eat many kinds of food, including rotting wood, insect larvae, and stored grain.

Darkling beetle 34

Click beetle

Up to 2¼ inches long
Beetle

These beetles get their name from the clicking sound they make as they leap in the air to right themselves after falling on their backs. They can jump as high as a foot.

Colorado beetle 36

Colorado beetle

Up to ⅜ inch long
Striped beetle

The Colorado beetle is a leaf eater. It is much feared by farmers, as adults and larvae can ruin potato plants, quickly reducing them to a blackened mess. They can be controlled with pesticides.

Rhinoceros beetle

¾ to 5 inches long
Beetle

This beetle can lift up to 850 times its own weight with its long horns. In the mating season, a male uses its horns as weapons in fights with rivals. The horns have spiny hairs to help grasp rivals.

Violin beetle 37

Violin beetle

1/16 to 1½ inches long
Beetle

Little is known about this strange-looking beetle. Its flattened body enables it to live wedged between layers of bracket fungi on the trunks of forest trees in Indonesia.

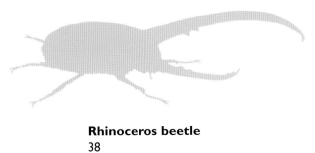

Rhinoceros beetle 38

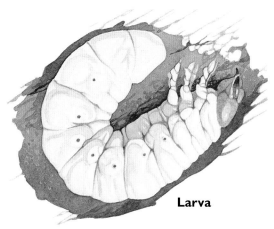

Larva

Larva and pupa

Stag beetle eggs hatch into wormlike, C-shaped larvae called grubs. They spend most of their time feeding and grow quickly. As a larva grows, it molts several times, shedding its skin to allow for the increase in body size. When the larva is fully grown, it becomes a pupa—the stage during which the larva changes into an adult beetle. When the process is complete, a winged, adult beetle comes out.

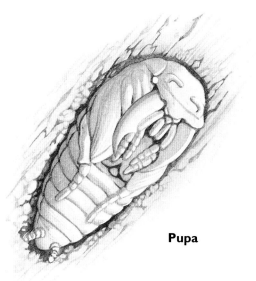

Pupa

Stag beetles

With their large heads and massive jaws, male stag beetles are among the most spectacular of all insects. But despite their fearsome appearance, these insects are harmless and feed mostly on tree sap and other liquids. There are about 1,250 species of stag beetles, some measuring up to 4 inches long. Stag beetles are black or brownish in color. They usually live in woodland and are particularly common in tropical areas.

The jaws of the male are like the antlers of a stag. Like stags, the males take part in fierce battles with one another to win the right to mate with females.

Female stag beetle

The female stag beetle is smaller than the battling male and does not have such large jaws. However, she can give a much more powerful nip if threatened. The male's mighty jaws are so specialized for fighting that they are almost useless for feeding or biting.

Its wing cases raised, this magnificent stag beetle is about to take to the air. When the beetle is not in flight, the tough wing cases, formed from the front wings, protect the more delicate back wings, which are folded underneath.

The helpless loser

If a stag beetle lands on its back after a battle, it is very hard for it to right itself again. In this position, it is extremely easy for other enemies, such as birds, to snap up the beetle.

Battling rivals

The beetles usually meet on the branch of a tree. As they struggle, each male tries to lock the other in its jaws—the jaws are just the right shape to fit around the top part of the rival stag beetle's body. Once one competitor succeeds in grabbing the other, he lifts the loser up and tries to throw him off the branch.

Grasshoppers, cockroaches, and relatives

These insects live everywhere, from the tops of mountains to city dwellings. While they are not closely related, they share certain features. All of them have strong jaws for chewing and most have large back wings. They also include some of the most ancient of all insect groups: cockroaches have existed on earth for 350 million years—early winged cockroaches may have been the first flying animals.

Most of these creatures are familiar to people, and some are even unwelcome guests in our homes.

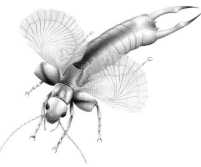

Long-horned earwig

Although they grow up to only 3 inches long, locusts can cause damage to crops wherever they swarm.

Cockroaches

Cockroaches are well-known indoor pests, although most live outdoors in every kind of habitat from mountains to rain forests. Cockroaches are fast runners—they are one of the fastest of all insects. All cockroaches have wings, but only a few can fly. They breed rapidly, carrying eggs in egg cases, which are attached to the female's body. Some egg cases are hidden in dark places soon after they are formed, while others remain attached to the body until shortly before they hatch.

German cockroach

¼ to ½ inch long
Cockroach

German cockroaches are found all over the world. They usually live indoors. They are fast runners and their flattened bodies are ideally shaped for squeezing into cracks and under floorboards.

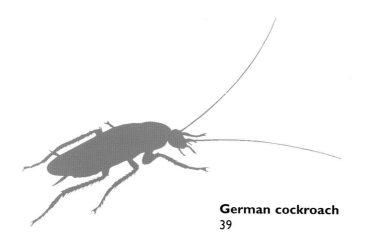

German cockroach
39

Madagascan hissing cockroach

2 to 3 inches long
Cockroach

These large, wingless cockroaches make a hissing sound through breathing holes in their abdomen to warn off enemies. Males also make a softer hissing noise when courting females.

Madagascan hissing cockroach
40

American cockroach

¾ to 2 inches long
Cockroach

The American cockroach is commonly found in buildings. It hides by day and feeds on anything it can find at night. The female lays her eggs in a case attached to her body and leaves the case in a dark, safe place before the eggs hatch.

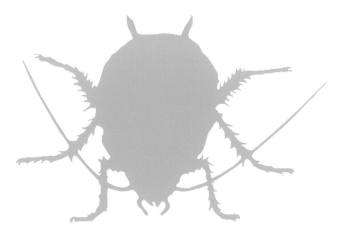

American cockroach
41

Harlequin cockroach

¾ to 2 inches long
Cockroach

Harlequin cockroaches live in Malaysia. The striking wing cases are shiny brown-black with yellow patches. A female harlequin cockroach lays a new egg case about every three days throughout her life.

Harlequin cockroach
42

Oriental cockroach
43

Oriental cockroach

1 to 1½ inches long
Cockroach

The oriental cockroach is a serious pest worldwide. It is often found in basements or in any damp areas of houses, such as under refrigerators and floors.

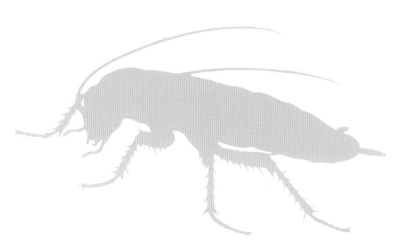

Metamorphosis

Insects go through several distinct growth stages before they become fully developed adults. This process is known as metamorphosis.

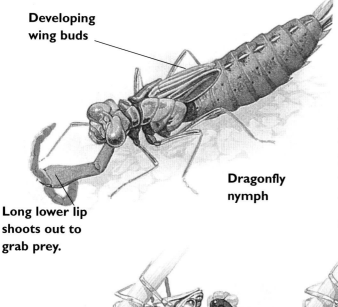

Developing wing buds

Long lower lip shoots out to grab prey.

Dragonfly nymph

Incomplete metamorphosis

The young of some insects, such as dragonflies, termites, true bugs, and cockroaches, are called nymphs. They hatch from eggs and look like small adult insects. They shed their skins about four to eight times as they mature. This slow transformation from young to adult is called incomplete metamorphosis.

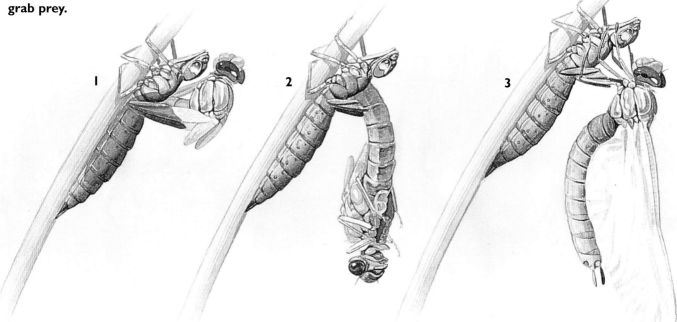

1

2

3

Skin of nymph splits and head and thorax of adult emerge.

The soft-bodied adult wriggles out of the old skin.

Adult waits for its wings and body to strengthen before flying away.

Complete metamorphosis

Insects such as butterflies and moths, flies, and wasps go through complete metamorphosis—this means a total body change. The larva (young) looks nothing like the adult. It molts several times and then becomes a pupa. Inside the pupa, the larva's body breaks down and a new, very different adult body forms.

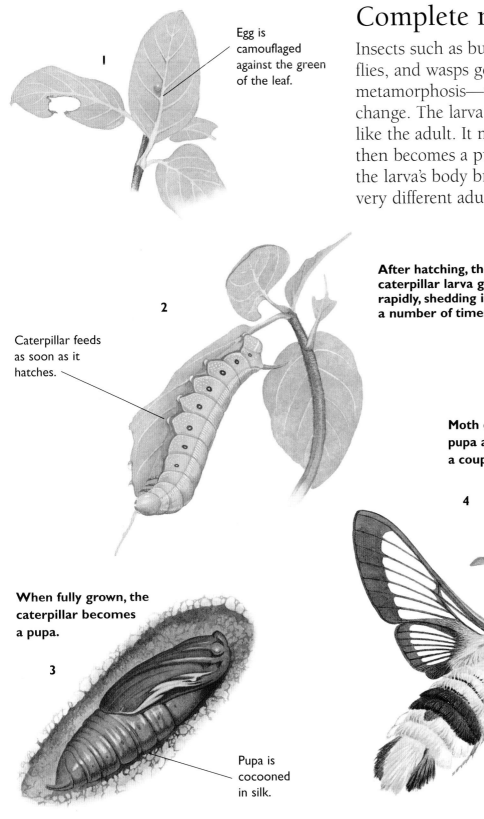

1

Egg is camouflaged against the green of the leaf.

2

Caterpillar feeds as soon as it hatches.

After hatching, the caterpillar larva grows rapidly, shedding its skin a number of times.

Moth emerges from pupa and can fly after a couple of hours.

4

When fully grown, the caterpillar becomes a pupa.

3

Pupa is cocooned in silk.

Earwigs and bristletails

Earwigs can look frightening because of their pincers, which they use to capture insect prey. But earwigs are harmless to human beings, and are usually welcomed by farmers because they catch other pests such as aphids. They feed on a wide variety of food, including both live and dead insects and live or decaying plants. Earwigs are active at night. During the day they hide in flower beds or under rocks or stones, or in dark places indoors. Also common in houses, but less often seen, are the wingless insects known as silverfish, usually found in kitchens and bathrooms.

Firebrat

⅓ to ¾ inch long
Earwig

The firebrat gets its name because it likes to live indoors near warm places such as fires, ovens, or boilers. It is a fast runner and scurries around finding crumbs and scraps of food to eat.

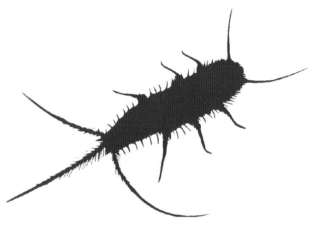

Firebrat
44

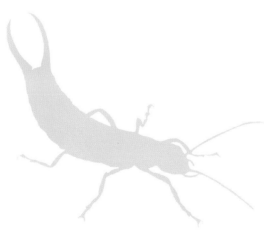

Common earwig
45

Common earwig

⅜ to 1 inch long
Earwig

The female earwig lays her eggs in a burrow and stays close to look after them. Unlike most insects, she cares for her young until they are able to look after themselves.

Long-horned earwig

⅜ to 1 inch long
Earwig

Like all earwigs, the long-horned earwig stays hidden during the day. It comes out at night to hunt other insects. If attacked by an enemy, it can scare it off by squirting a bad-smelling liquid from special glands on its abdomen. It has large, semicircular back wings that have to be folded many times in order to fit under the smaller, leathery front wings.

Long-horned earwig
46

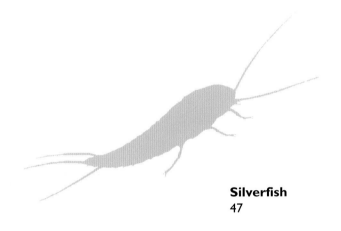

Silverfish
47

Silverfish

⅓ to ¾ inch long
Bristletail

Silverfish are fast movers. They usually live in dark corners indoors, where they avoid light. They eat paper, glue, and spilled foods. Their long bodies are covered with tiny scales.

Striped earwig

⅜ to 1 inch long
Earwig

The striped earwig has stripes running along its thorax. It is most common in tropical climates and is generally found in areas with sandy or clay soils. When crushed, this insect gives off a nasty smell.

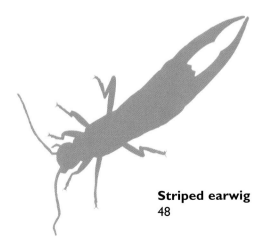

Striped earwig
48

Backyard play page

You can find the stickers of insects that live in gardens on pages 153–154. Stick them on this page to create your own backyard scene.

Grasshoppers, crickets, and relatives

Grasshoppers are more often heard than seen. Their high-pitched chirrups are usually made by males when courting females. They make these sounds by rubbing together special parts of their wings or legs. Crickets are relatives of grasshoppers and also make chirruping sounds. Phasmids are also relatives of grasshoppers. Some of them, called stick insects, look like twigs, and others, known as leaf insects, manage to look like leaves.

Bush katydid
49

Bush katydid

½ to 3 inches long
Grasshopper

These insects are also known as bush crickets. They have wings that look amazingly like leaves and are usually colored to camouflage with the plants that the katydids live on. Some wings resemble dead leaves or are colored like lichen or bark.

Short-horned grasshopper

½ to 3 inches long
Grasshopper

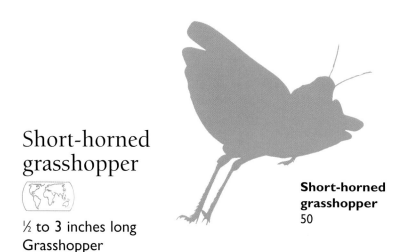

Short-horned grasshopper
50

Short-horned grasshoppers are so called because they have short antennae. Like all grasshoppers, they have powerful back legs and can leap more than 200 times their own length.

Long-horned grasshopper

½ to 3 inches long
Grasshopper

As their name suggests, long-horned grasshoppers have long antennae. They feed on plants but also catch and eat small insects. Many are green or brown in color and can be hard to spot in the trees and bushes where they live.

Long-horned grasshopper
51

Leaf insect

2 to 4 inches long
Phasmid

These extraordinary insects resemble the leaves they live on, complete with "veins." Even their eggs look like the seeds of the plant it lives on. Leaf insects live in tropical parts of Asia and Australia.

Leaf insect
52

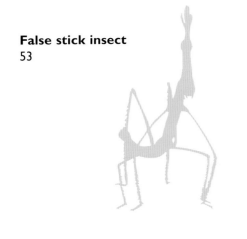

False stick insect
53

False stick insect

Up to 4 inches long
Grasshopper

This bizarre-looking insect is really a grasshopper. It fools its enemies into mistaking it for a twig. False stick insects live in trees, bushes, and plants in tropical rain forests and semidesert areas.

Locust

½ to 3 inches long
Grasshopper

Locusts are a type of grasshopper and are among the most damaging of all insects. Swarms of locusts swoop down onto crops and feed until there are scarcely any leaves left. A swarm may contain as many as 50 billion insects.

Locust
54

Katydid

½ to 3 inches long
Grasshopper

The katydid gets its name from its song, which sounds like "katy-did, katy-didn't" chirped over and over. The katydid has wings that look like leaves to help it hide among plants. The female has a knifelike ovipositor (egg-laying tube). She uses this to insert eggs into slots that she cuts in the stems of plants.

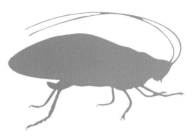

Katydid
55

Tree cricket
56

Tree cricket

⅜ to 1 inch long
Cricket

Tree crickets "sing" by rubbing together thickened areas of their front wings to make a high-pitched sound. They are usually colored green, black, or brown. Tree crickets have broad bodies and feelers at the end of their abdomen. They also have "ears" just below the knees on their forelegs, so that they can hear the mating songs of other crickets.

Mole cricket

¾ to 2 inches long
Cricket

Like tiny moles, these crickets live under the ground. They burrow with their large, spadelike front legs. A covering of fine hairs protects their body from soil. Plant roots are their main food, but they also eat worms and larvae.

Mole cricket
57

Stick insect

Up to 1 foot long
Phasmid

With its slender green or brown body, the stick insect looks so much like a leafless twig that it is hard for hungry birds to see. During the day it clings to a plant. At night it moves around, feeding on leaves.

Desert locust

Up to 3 inches long
Grasshopper

From time to time, if their numbers increase a lot or food becomes scarce, locusts that normally live alone will form a swarm—a large group of insects. Huge swarms then fly hundreds of miles, destroying crops as they go.

Desert locust
60

Stick insect
58

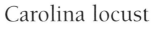

Carolina locust

1⅜ to 2 inches long
Grasshopper

This locust can do lots of damage to food crops. Its color camouflages it in its natural habitat of dry fields and grasses.

Carolina locust
59

Spur-throated grasshopper

1 to 1⅜ inches long
Grasshopper

This grasshopper is very common in fields and prairies, where there are plenty of plants to eat. It eats leaves and flowers so quickly that it can cause great damage to food crops.

Spur-throated grasshopper
61

51

Eggs and egg laying

After mating, insects lay their eggs. The eggs will hatch into young insects, so they need protection from predators. A young insect develops inside its egg until it is ready to hatch.

Male

Male grips female with his abdomen.

Female

Damselflies

Many bugs, such as damselflies, lay their eggs in or close to water. Soon after she has mated, a female damselfly positions herself on the stem of a water plant and places her eggs below the waterline. The male, still flying, guards her and holds her steady while she is laying her eggs.

Queen and worker ant

Worker removes egg laid by queen.

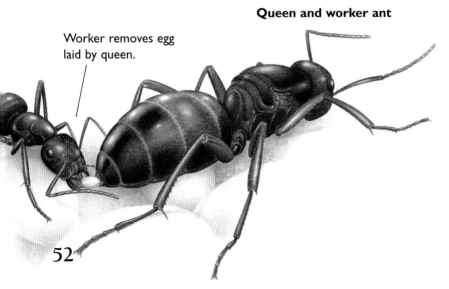

Carpenter ant

Ants live in huge, well-organized groups called colonies. Most of the ants in the colony are female worker ants. Each colony includes a queen ant, who lays all the eggs after mating with the few male ants in the colony. Worker ants look after the eggs in special nest chambers.

Ichneumon wasp

Insect parents often make sure that their young will have a meal ready for them when they hatch. The female ichneumon wasp listens for the vibrations of a wood-boring beetle larva in a tree trunk. She drills into the wood with her egg-laying tube and lays an egg on the body of the larva. The newly hatched ichneumon will feed on the juicy larva.

The egg-laying tube is known as an ovipositor.

The ovipositor is longer than the ichneumon's whole body.

Spider egg sacs

Spiders lay their eggs and then wrap them in silk to form an egg sac. This may then be attached to a leaf or other surface. Some spiders carry their egg sacs around to protect them. In some species, the egg sac contains just a single egg, in others as many as 3,000. The female guards her eggs until they hatch.

A female spider carries her large, white egg sac to protect it.

53

Dragonflies, mantids, and relatives

The insects in this chapter include some of the fiercest predators in the insect world. Mantids are well known for their expert hunting methods. They have long front legs, which they extend at lightning speed to grasp their prey.

Dragonflies are more energetic hunters. They are some of the fastest-flying of all insects. They seize their prey in the air or pluck tiny creatures from leaves. Like the slower-flying damselflies and mayflies, dragonflies spend much of their life as nymphs (young dragonflies). The nymphs are hunters, too. They catch prey in their strong jaws.

A slender mantis sits poised on a branch, ready to catch any unwary victim that comes too close.

Narrow-winged damselfly

Mantids and relatives

Mantids can fold their two pairs of wings like a roof over their body. Their larvae hatch as tiny versions of their parents and start hunting for themselves right away. Newly hatched mantids even eat one another.

Angola mantis

½ to 6 inches long
Mantis

This mantis is hard to see as it lies on a lichen-covered branch. It remains very still while it watches for food but can reach out to grab its prey in a fraction of a second.

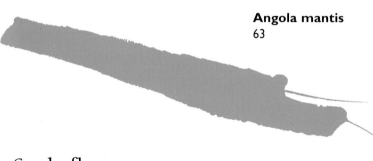

Angola mantis
63

Snakefly

½ to 1 inch long
Mantis

The snakefly gets its name from its long, snakelike neck, which it lifts as it searches for prey. Both adults and larvae hunt insects such as aphids and caterpillars.

56

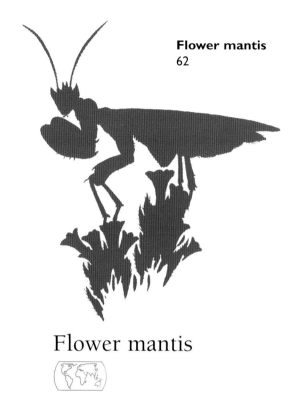

Flower mantis
62

Flower mantis

½ to 6 inches long
Mantis

The flower mantis is colored to match the flowers that it perches on. This helps it stay hidden from both its victims and its enemies. It usually preys on other insects but it can also catch frogs and small lizards.

Snakefly
64

Mantisfly

⅛ to 1 inch long
Mantis

The mantisfly looks like a small praying mantis and catches prey in the same way. Some mantisfly larvae burrow into the nests of wasps or bees and eat their larvae. Others feed on spider eggs.

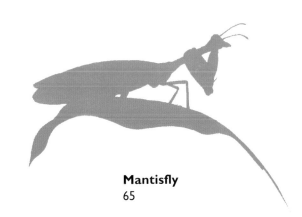

Mantisfly
65

Common stone fly

⅜ to 1½ inches long
Stone fly

The stone fly nymphs (young) live in streams. They feed mostly on plants, although some hunt insects. Adult stone flies are poor fliers and spend much of the day resting. Adults live only two or three weeks and most do not feed.

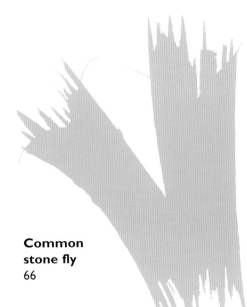

Common stone fly
66

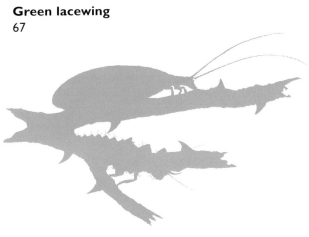

Green lacewing
67

Green lacewing

⅜ to ¾ inch long
Lacewing

Adult lacewings and their larvae feed on small insects such as aphids. The larvae suck out the body juices of their prey with their special mouthparts.

57

Self-defense

Just as many insects are predators, insects themselves are hunted and eaten by many other animals—including other insects. Because of this, insects and arachnids have a wide range of methods of self-defense, from stings, bites, and poison sprays to playing dead.

Bombardier beetle

Some species of beetle use poisonous chemicals to keep predators away. If an attacker is not put off by the bombardier's bright warning colors, the beetle swivels its abdomen around to fire a spray of boiling-hot chemicals into the attacker's face.

Huge jaws make effective weapons.

Poison is forced out of the beetle's body with a loud "pop."

Army ant

Sometimes attack is the best form of defense. The jaws of army ants are among the insect world's most impressive defense mechanisms. Platoons of army ants will attack and bite any intruder, often killing it.

Only the male giraffe-necked weevils have long necks, but no one is quite sure why.

Giraffe-necked weevil

This curious-looking insect gets its name from its incredibly long neck. It has a smart way of avoiding being eaten. If attacked, it rolls over and pretends to be dead until the danger passes. Many carnivores feed only on live flesh, so they leave the weevil alone.

Funnel-web spider

Adopting a threatening posture will sometimes deter attackers. If caught in the open, a funnel-web spider takes up an aggressive pose, raising its front legs and exposing its fearsome fangs. Some insects, such as the cricketlike wetas, scare off enemies by making alarming noises.

The funnel-web's venom can kill a person.

59

Pond play page

You can find the stickers of insects that live in
ponds on pages 155–156. Stick them on this page
to create your own pond scene.

Dragonflies and relatives

Dragonflies have long bodies and two pairs of see-through wings. They are some of the fastest-flying insects. They seize their prey in the air or pluck tiny creatures from leaves. They are found near rivers, streams, lakes, and ponds. Their young (called larvae or nymphs) live in the water. The adults have big eyes, made up of thousands of separate parts, giving the insect excellent eyesight for catching its prey.

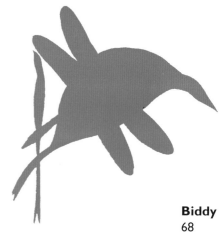

Biddy
68

Biddy

2¼ to 3¼ inches long
Dragonfly

Biddies are large dragonflies often seen over woodland streams, where they hover about 12 inches above the surface. They are usually brownish and have big eyes. Biddy nymphs are large and live at the bottom of streams, feeding on insects and tadpoles.

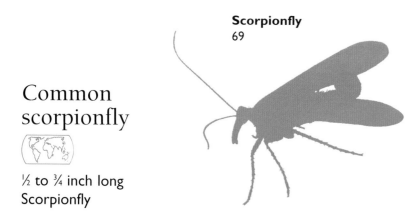

Scorpionfly
69

Common scorpionfly

½ to ¾ inch long
Scorpionfly

This insect gets its name from the curving end of the male's body, which looks like a scorpion's stinger. It eats nectar and fruit as well as insects.

Damselfly

About ⅜ inch long
Damselfly

These insects are sometimes known as spread-winged damselflies because they hold their wings partly spread out when at rest. They live around ponds and marshes, where they catch insects such as small flies.

Damselfly
70

62

Clubtail dragonfly

2 to 3 inches long
Dragonfly

These dragonflies hunt in a different way from many other dragonflies. The clubtail finds a suitable perch and watches for prey. Once it sights a victim, it darts out to seize it, then returns to the perch to eat.

Clubtail dragonfly
71

Skimmer

¾ to 2½ inches long
Dragonfly

A skimmer is a kind of dragonfly with a wide, flattened body that is shorter than its wingspan. Some have wingspans of up to 4 inches. Skimmers are usually seen flying near still or slow-moving water, such as ponds and swamps.

Skimmer
73

Darter

¾ to 2½ inches long
Dragonfly

This type of dragonfly gets its name from its fast, darting flight. Like all dragonflies, darters lay their eggs in or close to water. The young look very different from the adults and live in water, catching prey such as tadpoles.

Darter
75

Narrow-winged damselfly

1 to 2 inches long
Damselfly

The males of these damselflies are usually brighter in color than the females. Their nymphs, like those of all damselflies, live in water and catch small insects to eat.

Narrow-winged damselfly
72

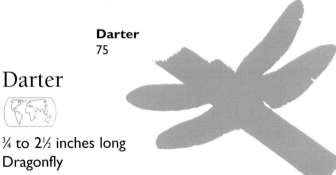

Emperor dragonfly
74

Emperor dragonfly

2½ to 5 inches long
Dragonfly

The emperor dragonfly's wings are up to 5 inches long. Like many dragonflies, a male emperor usually has a territory that he patrols and defends. He allows female mates to enter the territory but chases away rival males.

Finding a mate

Like other animals, male and female insects and spiders mate to produce young. Many bugs use scent to find mates of the right species, but others use sounds, displays, lights, or even gifts.

Fireflies

While many insects use chemical signals to attract mates, fireflies use light. Male fireflies fly through the night sky flashing lights from their abdomens to attract females. A female signals that she is ready to mate by flashing back. Each firefly species has its own pattern of flashing.

Groups of male fireflies may flash their lights all at the same time.

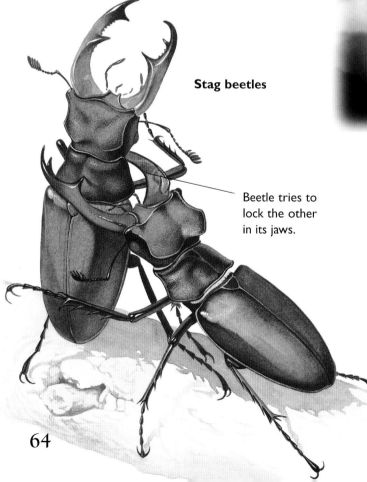

Stag beetles

Beetle tries to lock the other in its jaws.

Stag beetles

Male insects will sometimes fight with each other over the right to mate with a female. Rival male stag beetles battle with their large, antlerlike jaws. The larger beetle usually wins by flipping its rival onto its back. The loser finds it hard to get upright again.

Dragonflies

When dragonflies mate, the male grips the neck of the female with the tip of his abdomen. The female then bends her own abdomen up, forming a heart shape. She collects sperm from the lower part of his abdomen to fertilize her eggs.

Male

Female

Female collects sperm from the male.

The pair mate while they are either at rest or in flight.

Spiders

A female spider attracts a male using a special scent called a pheromone. To avoid being mistaken for prey and eaten by the female, a male spider may pluck at her web in a special way or perform a dance. Some species of spiders offer their females gifts of food or tie them up with silk when mating.

65

Flies, moths, and butterflies

Everywhere in the world that plants grow, there are butterflies and moths. The young butterfly or moth is called a caterpillar and spends most of its life feeding and growing. When it reaches full size, it becomes a pupa. During this stage, it makes its transformation from wingless larva to winged adult.

One of the largest groups of insects, flies are common almost everywhere. Some flies, such as mosquitoes and black flies, suck blood from humans and other animals. Flies are thought of as disease carriers, but they do have their value. Like bees, they pollinate plants as they feed. They are also a source of food for many other creatures, such as birds. Flies feed on waste, such as dung and dead animal bodies, helping to get rid of it.

Monarch butterflies feeding. This species is native to North and South America.

Housefly

67

Flies

There are more than 90,000 known species of flies worldwide. Flies only have one pair of wings to fly with. They also have small, knobbly organs called halteres, which help them keep their balance while in flight.

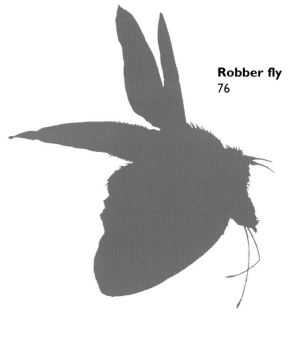

**Robber fly
76**

Horsefly

¼ to 1 inch long
True fly

These flies have large, shimmering eyes. Males feed on pollen and nectar, but female horseflies take blood from mammals, including horses and humans. Their bites can be painful and the flies may carry diseases such as anthrax.

**Horsefly
77**

Robber fly

¼ to 1¾ inches long
True fly

The robber fly is a fast-moving hunter. It chases and catches other insects in the air or pounces on them on the ground. It has strong, bristly legs for seizing its prey. Once it has caught its victim, the robber fly sucks out its body fluids.

Nonbiting midge

¹⁄₁₆ to ⅜ inch long
Gnat

Midges are tiny, delicate insects that fly in huge swarms, usually in the evening, often near ponds and streams. There are two families of midges: those that do not bite, and those that bite other animals, including humans.

**Nonbiting midge
78**

Crane fly

1/4 to 2 1/4 inches long
True fly

With their long, thin legs, crane flies look like large mosquitoes, but they do not bite or suck blood. The largest have a wingspan of as much as 3 inches. Most adults live only a few days and probably do not eat at all.

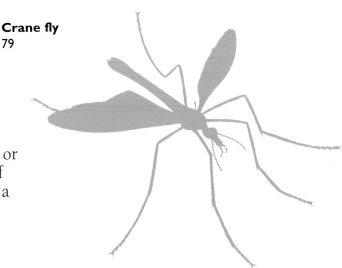

Crane fly
79

Hover fly
80

Hover fly

1/4 to 1 1/4 inches long
True fly

Adult hover flies feed on pollen and nectar and are also known as flower flies. They can hover with ease and even fly backward. Many species are brightly colored and look much like bees or wasps. They do not sting, however.

Biting midge

1/16 to 1/4 inch long
Gnat

Swarms of these tiny midges gather on warm evenings near ponds and lakes. Some are predators, using sharp mouthparts to suck animals' blood or other body fluids.

Biting midge
81

Blowfly

¼ to ⅜ inch long
True fly

Many blowflies are colored metallic blue or green. They often lay their eggs in carrion—the bodies of dead animals—or in dung. The larvae, called maggots, have plenty of food to eat when they hatch.

Blowfly
82

Housefly
83

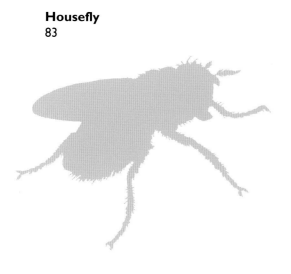

Housefly

⅛ to ½ inch long
True fly

Houseflies are found almost everywhere in the world. They suck liquids from manure and other decaying matter and from fresh fruit and plants. In some places they carry diseases, such as cholera and typhoid fever.

Fruit fly

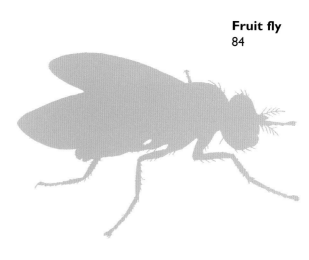

⅛ to ⅜ inch long
True fly

These little flies are common around flowers and overripe fruit. Their larvae feed on plant matter and some are serious pests, causing great damage to fruit trees and other crops.

Fruit fly
84

Dance fly

⅜ inch long
True fly

Dance flies have a long, straight proboscis. When they gather in swarms, they bob up and down in a dancelike flight. Females feed on flowers, but males hunt insects. During courtship, a male may give a female a dead insect as a "wedding present."

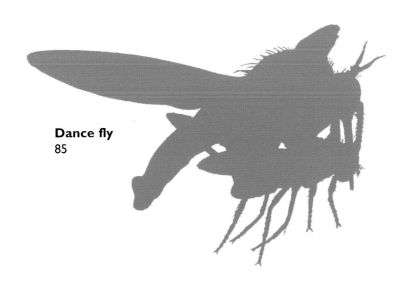

Dance fly
85

Black fly

Up to ¼ inch long
True fly

These stout-bodied flies have a humped back, which is why they are also called buffalo flies. Males feed on flower nectar, but most females are bloodsuckers, taking food from mammals and birds.

Black fly
86

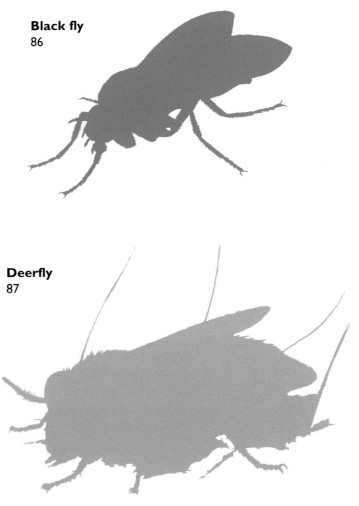

Deerfly

Up to 1⅛ inches long
True fly

Deerflies are bloodsucking insects related to horseflies but a little smaller. They can give painful bites to horses, cattle, and humans. Some species can even carry dangerous diseases such as anthrax.

Deerfly
87

Mosquitoes

Mosquitoes are usually heard before they are seen. Their wings beat so fast—about 500 beats a second—that the insects make a constant whining sound as they fly. There are about 3,000 different species of these slender, long-legged flies. Although there are more species in warmer areas near the equator, the greatest swarms are found in the far north during the brief Arctic summer.

Feeding

Male, and sometimes female, mosquitoes feed on nectar and plant sap. Most females also bite and suck the blood of vertebrate animals—they need the protein-rich food so that they can produce eggs. In one meal the female can take in twice her own weight in blood. Mosquitoes are most active at dusk and at night, but each species has its own time of activity and some species bite during the day.

A blood meal

To feed on blood, the mosquito pierces the host's skin with its special tubelike mouthparts. It then pumps some saliva into the wound to keep the blood flowing as it sucks. This saliva is what makes the bite itch.

Mosquito life cycle

Most mosquitoes deposit their eggs in water, where they float on the surface, or on aquatic plants. Some species lay single eggs; others lay groups of eggs called rafts. The eggs hatch into aquatic larvae, which feed on particles in the water. The larvae then become pupae, and a few days later an adult mosquito emerges from each pupal case.

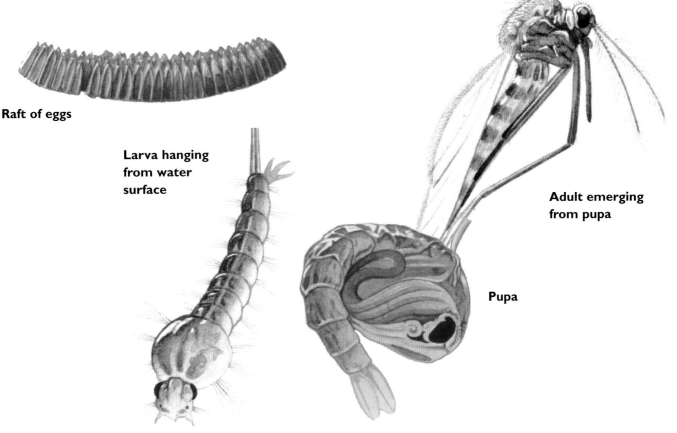

Raft of eggs

Larva hanging from water surface

Pupa

Adult emerging from pupa

Disease carrier

Certain mosquito species carry tiny parasites in their bodies that cause an illness called malaria. These parasites enter the host's blood when the mosquito bites.

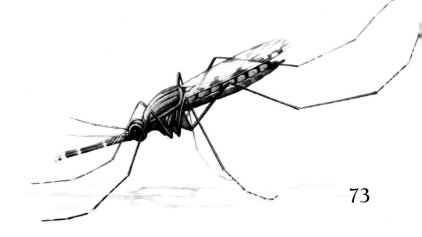

73

Woodland play page

You can find the stickers of insects that live in forests on pages 156–157. Stick them on this page to create your own woodland scene.

Moths

Moths and butterflies belong to the same family but there are a few differences between them. Moths have shorter antennae and usually rest with their wings open, unlike butterflies. The antennae help male moths pick up the scent signals given off by females when looking for mates. Adults often do not feed during their short lives. Moths are generally active by night, but butterflies are mostly active by day.

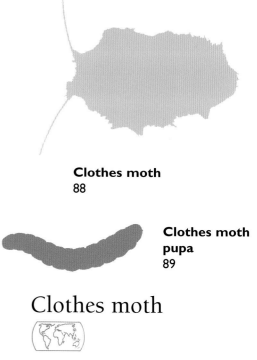

Clothes moth
88

Geometrid moth
90

Clothes moth pupa
89

Geometrid moth

½ to 1½ inches (wingspan)
Moth

Geometrid caterpillars are known as inchworms or "loopers" because of the loop shape they make as they move. They eat leaves and can cause serious damage to trees.

Clothes moth

½ to ¾ inch (wingspan)
Moth

Adult clothes moths are small and brownish. In the wild the caterpillars feed on hair and feathers in animal nests or on small dead animals. In our homes the caterpillars feed on the wool in clothes.

Geometrid moth caterpillar
91

Hummingbird moth

1½ to 6 inches (wingspan)
Moth

This moth hovers as it feeds, reaching its long proboscis, or feeding tube, deep into flowers for their nectar. It makes a noise a little like the sound of a hummingbird's wings.

Hummingbird moth
92

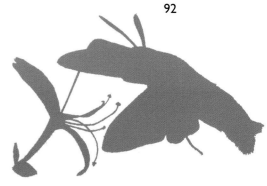

Atlas moth

1 to 10 inches (wingspan)
Moth

These brightly patterned moths are some of the largest in the world. Most have feathery antennae and transparent patches on their broad wings where there are no scales.

Atlas moth
93

Tiger moth

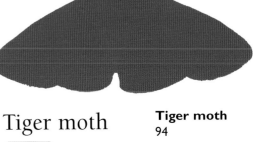

Tiger moth
94

¾ to 2¾ inches (wingspan)
Moth

Tiger moths have broad, hairy bodies and bold patterns on their wings that warn predators that they do not taste good.

Large caddis fly

½ to 1 inch (wingspan)
Moth

Large caddis fly caterpillar
96

Caddis flies look like moths but have hair instead of scales on their bodies and wings. They also have short mouthparts for lapping up food.

Large caddis fly
95

Cotton boll moth

Cotton boll moth
97

½ to 3 inches (wingspan)
Moth

The cotton boll moth belongs to one of the biggest families of moths. Most fly at night and are dull in color. The caterpillar feeds on cotton seedpods and can damage the plants.

Luna moth

Luna moth
98

1 to 10 inches (wingspan)
Moth

This beautiful moth has huge wings with long tails trailing from them. It lives in forests and its caterpillars feed on the leaves of trees such as hickory, walnut, and birch.

Sphinx moths

Of all butterflies and moths, sphinx moths, also called hawk moths, are some of the most powerful fliers. Their wings beat so fast that they make a whirring noise. The moths can even hover like hummingbirds in front of flowers as they feed. There are about 1,200 species of sphinx moths, some with wingspans of up to 6 inches. Most have large, heavy bodies and long, narrow front wings.

Bee sphinx moth

A bee sphinx moth plunges its long tongue deep into a flower. With its broad, striped body and the large, clear areas without scales on its wings, this moth looks amazingly like a bee as it hovers over plants. It flies by day, not at night.

Egg to adult

As soon as a caterpillar hatches from its egg, it starts to feed on plants. It grows fast and sheds its skin several times as it gets bigger. When fully grown, the caterpillar becomes a pupa. As it passes through this stage, it stays on the ground in a cocoon made of silk. When it comes out from its cocoon, the adult sphinx moth, like all moths, eats liquid food such as plant nectar. It sucks up the food with a special kind of tongue called a proboscis. The proboscis is hollow in the middle, like a drinking straw, and is kept rolled up under the head when not in use. Sphinx moths have the longest tongues of any moths.

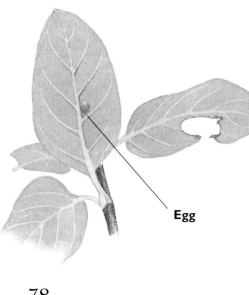

Egg

Caterpillar

Bee sphinx moth pupa in cocoon

Poplar sphinx moth

The color and unusual shape of the poplar sphinx moth's wings help it to hide on bark as it rests during the day. Its caterpillars feed on the leaves of trees such as poplar and willow.

Adult

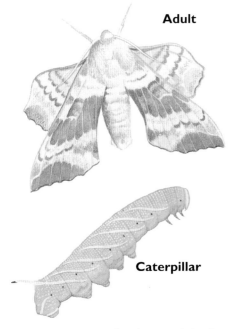

Caterpillar

Oleander sphinx moth

Adult

This is one of the most beautifully patterned of all moths. Its caterpillar feeds on the leaves of plants such as oleander and grows up to 6 inches long. It has bold eyespots on its body, which can fool a predator into thinking it a much larger creature than it really is.

Caterpillar

A privet moth lands on a flower to feed on nectar with the help of its long proboscis. The moth's caterpillar feeds on the leaves of privet, lilac, and ash.

White-lined sphinx moth

The white-lined sphinx moth visits flowers at night to feed. Like most moths, it has antennae that pick up smells as well as being used to touch objects. It uses its antennae to help it find flowers in the darkness.

79

Butterflies

Everywhere in the world that plants grow, there are butterflies. This is the second largest group of insects, with about 150,000 species. A butterfly or moth larva is called a caterpillar. It spends most of its life eating plants and growing fast. When it has reached its full size, a caterpillar becomes a pupa, wrapping itself in a case called a cocoon. During this stage it changes from wingless larva to winged adult.

Fluminense swallowtail butterfly

2 to 11 inches (wingspan)
Butterfly

This beautiful butterfly is one of Brazil's most endangered insects. Its swampy, bushy habitat has been used to build houses and factories and this has caused it to die out in many sites.

Morpho butterfly

1 to 4¼ inches (wingspan)
Butterfly

**Morpho
100**

Morpho butterflies live in the rain forests of Central and South America. The males are brilliantly colored. They have rows of scales on their wings that are mirrorlike. Females are much plainer.

Cairns birdwing butterfly

2 to 11 inches (wingspan)
Butterfly

Cairns birdwings, like all birdwings, are found only in Southeast Asia and northern Australia. Females are bigger than males, but males are more colorful. Birdwings, which are the biggest butterflies in the world, are highly prized by collectors and many are now rare.

Swallowtail butterfly

**Swallowtail
101**

2 to 11 inches (wingspan)
Butterfly

Boldly patterned swallowtail butterflies get their name from the tail-like extensions on their back wings. These may help to distract enemies away from their sensitive head area.

**Cairns birdwing
102**

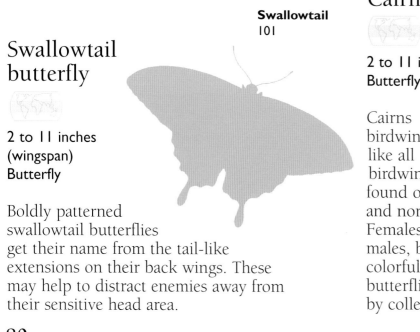

80

Copper butterfly

Copper
103

1 to 2 inches (wingspan)
Butterfly

These little butterflies have brightly colored wings. When at rest or feeding on flowers, they hold their wings together at the back. The caterpillars are fat and sluglike in shape. They feed on the leaves of weedy plants.

Copper caterpillar
104

Cabbage white butterfly

¾ to 2¾ inches (wingspan)
Butterfly

Cabbage white caterpillar
106

The cabbage white is a very common butterfly. Unlike many butterflies, cabbage whites have well-developed front legs, which are used for walking. Their caterpillars eat cabbage and other leafy crops and can do great damage.

Cabbage white
105

Monarch
107

Monarch butterfly

¼ to 1¼ inches (wingspan)
Butterfly

Every fall, millions of monarch butterflies fly south from Canada and the northern United States to California and Mexico—a distance of about 2,000 miles. The following spring, the butterflies fly north again.

Queen Alexandra's birdwing
108

Queen Alexandra's birdwing butterfly

2 to 11 inches (wingspan)
Butterfly

The female of this species is the biggest butterfly in the world.

Camouflage, mimicry, and warnings

Insects provide tasty meals for all kinds of other creatures. One way of avoiding being eaten by predators is to remain hidden from view, using shape and coloring to blend perfectly into the background. This is called camouflage. Mimicking insects scare predators away by copying the shape, coloring, and behavior of dangerous animals. Other insects have warning colors to trick predators into thinking that they are poisonous to eat.

Treehoppers gather in large groups.

The "thorn" on its back almost covers its wings.

Treehopper

Hugging a branch tightly, the treehopper bug is of no interest to hungry birds. The strange shape on its thorax makes it look like a sharp thorn.

Leaf insect

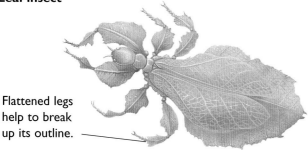

Flattened legs help to break up its outline.

Leaf insect

Sitting on a bush, this insect, with its leaf-shaped wings and their veinlike markings, is almost invisible. A leaf insect can change its color, becoming darker at night and paler by day.

Lichen spider

The lichen spider sits head-downward on a lichen-covered tree trunk. When danger threatens, it flattens itself against the tree bark. The spider's mottled coloring and the hairy tufts on its legs disguise it against the bark. The hairs also help to keep the spider's legs from casting clear shadows.

Colors blend in with lichen.

Stick insect

A stick insect's slender body is almost impossible to tell apart from a leafless twig. In daylight, it clings to a plant and remains very still. It uses its camouflage to avoid the attention of birds.

Oil beetle

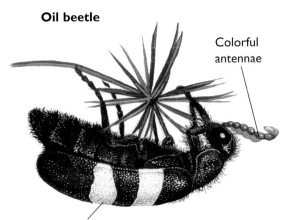

Colorful antennae

To a predator, the bright yellow bands say "this insect tastes horrible."

Luna moth

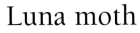

The luna moth tricks birds with its false-eye spots. When a bird sees the flashing "eyes" on the moth's wings, it mistakes them for the eyes of one of its own enemies and backs off.

Oil beetle

The leg joints of this beetle contain a foul-tasting oil that protects it from predators. The oil contains a substance that causes blisters (which is why oil beetles are also called blister beetles).

Saddleback caterpillar

A plump, slow-moving caterpillar makes a tempting snack for a passing bird. Rather than use camouflage to hide from predators, the saddleback caterpillar has a colorful patch on its back. This warns birds that it is poisonous and best left alone.

White is a warning color for predators.

The tufts of short, poisonous bristles sting would-be predators.

Hoverfly

Predators often mistake this yellow-and-black striped fly for a wasp, and steer clear to avoid its venomous sting. The hoverfly is actually stingless, but it mimics the coloring and shape of wasps to fool predators.

A hoverfly has only one pair of wings, unlike a wasp, which has two.

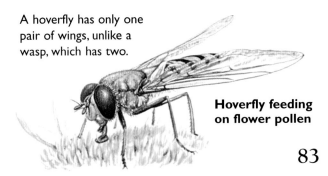

Hoverfly feeding on flower pollen

83

Bees, wasps, ants, and termites

Bees, wasps, and ants belong to a large group of insects known as hymenopterans. Most have a "waist" at the front of their abdomen. They have chewing mouthparts and tonguelike structures for sucking liquids from flowers. While most hymenopterans live alone, ants and some bees and wasps live in colonies. Usually, a colony is headed by a queen—the only female to mate and lay eggs. Other females build the nest, gather food, and care for the young. The few males in a colony do not work and are present only at certain times of the year to mate with the queen.

Termites are similar to hymenopterans but belong to a separate group called isopterans. They are small insects that live in huge colonies in nests. These nests are made in wood, soil, trees, or in specially built mounds.

Leaf-cutter ant

A honeybee fills her pollen baskets with a flower's pollen. She will return to her colony with her load.

Social insects

Some insects, such as termites, bees, ants, and wasps, live in huge groups called colonies. Usually, a single female queen lays all the eggs, while worker insects run the colony.

Termite mound

"Chimney" lets air in and out and controls the temperature inside.

The mound is built from soil and termite saliva.

Termite mound

Of all insect nests, a termite mound is the most spectacular, rising up to nearly 16 feet high. Inside these mounds is a maze of tunnels and chambers. Some chambers are food stores, others are nurseries for looking after eggs and young, and there is even a royal chamber for the queen termite—the head of the colony.

More than a million termites live in the nest.

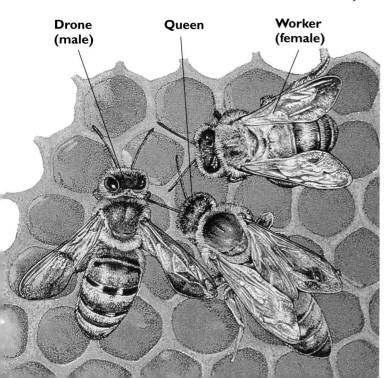

Drone (male)

Queen

Worker (female)

Bee honeycomb

The honeybee builds its nest from wax that it makes in its own body. The nest consists of sheets of hexagonal cells. Each sheet is called a comb. Eggs are laid in some cells, and food, such as pollen or honey, is stored in others.

Termites grow fungi to eat.

Paper wasp nest

Paper wasp nest

A queen paper wasp builds a nest on her own. She makes a series of papery envelopes out of chewed-up wood mixed with saliva. She then lays her eggs in the envelopes. Later, other females arrive to help her feed her newly hatched larvae with insects.

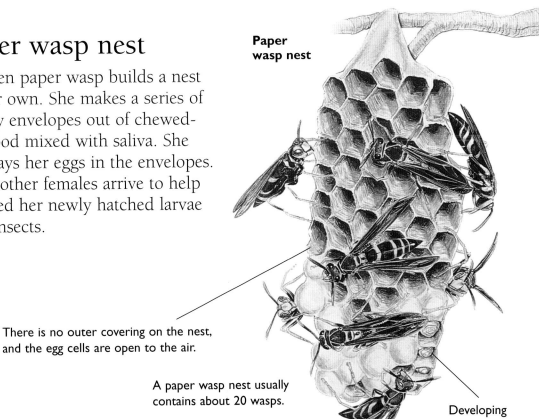

There is no outer covering on the nest, and the egg cells are open to the air.

A paper wasp nest usually contains about 20 wasps.

Developing larvae

Weaver ants

These ants make nests in trees. A row of worker ants pulls two leaves together. Other workers hold ant larvae with their jaws. They use the ant larvae to produce silk. The ants use the silk to "sew" together the leaf edges. The finished nest is a ball or column of leaves.

Weaver ants at work

87

Bees

Some bees live alone and make their own nests for their young. Others live in colonies that may contain thousands of bees. The bumblebee is a good example of these "social" bees. When the queen starts a new hive in spring, she collects pollen and nectar and makes food called beebread. After her larvae hatch, they feed on the beebread as they grow to become worker bees. These larvae become adult worker bees and they take over the work of the colony while the queen continues to lay eggs.

Leaf-cutter bee
109

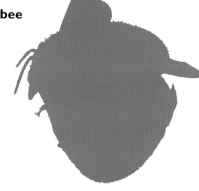

Leaf-cutter bee

⅜ to ¾ inch long
Bee

The leaf-cutter bee cuts circular pieces from leaves and flowers with its jaws and uses them to line cells in its nest. It stores nectar and pollen in each cell and lays an egg in each one.

Bumblebee

Bumblebee
110

⅛ to 1 inch long
Bee

Bumblebees are large and covered in hair. The queen is the only member of a bumblebee hive to live through the winter. In spring she looks for a new underground nest site.

Plasterer bee

Plasterer bee
111

⅛ to ¾ inch long
Bee

Plasterer bees nest in burrows with branching tunnels. They line the tunnels with a liquid produced by glands in their abdomens. This substance dries to become clear and waterproof.

Orchid bee

Orchid bee
112

⅛ to 1 inch long
Bee

Most orchid bees live in tropical areas and are brightly colored. Males are attracted to orchid flowers for their nectar. They pollinate the flowers and collect scent from them. This scent may play a part in their mating rituals.

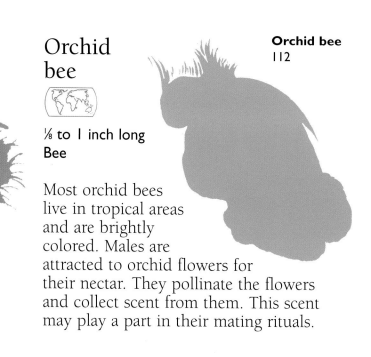

Carpenter bee

⅛ to 1 inch long
Bee

The female carpenter bee chews a tunnel-like nest in wood. She makes a line of cells inside the tunnel, fills each cell with food stores of pollen and nectar, and lays one egg in each cell. She stays nearby and guards the nest against enemies.

Stingless bee

⅛ to 1 inch long
Bee

Although these bees cannot sting, they have strong jaws with which they can bite any intruders. They live in colonies in nests that they make under the ground, in a tree trunk, or even in part of a termites' nest.

Carpenter bee
113

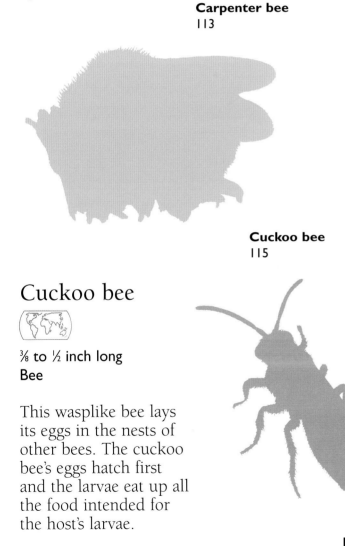

Stingless bee
114

Cuckoo bee
115

Mining bee

⅛ to ¾ inch long
Bee

Mining bees nest in long, branching tunnels, which they dig in the ground. Each bee digs its own nest but large numbers may live close together.

Cuckoo bee

⅜ to ½ inch long
Bee

This wasplike bee lays its eggs in the nests of other bees. The cuckoo bee's eggs hatch first and the larvae eat up all the food intended for the host's larvae.

Mining bee
116

Honeybees

Of all the many types of bees, honeybees are probably the best known. They pollinate countless food crops and produce millions of dollars' worth of honey and wax every year.

Colonies

Many bees lead solitary lives, but honeybees live in huge colonies of thousands of bees. Each colony has a queen. The queen bee is larger than the other bees and lays all the eggs of the colony. Most of the members of the colony are female workers. The nest is made in a hollow tree or in a hive made up of six-sided cells, provided by a human beekeeper. These cells contain eggs and young as well as food stores of pollen and honey.

Workers

A worker honeybee lives only about six weeks. For the first week of her adult life she cares for the eggs and larvae of the colony. Then she helps to build cells and maintain the nest. Finally she becomes a food gatherer, bringing nectar and pollen back to the nest.

Worker bees

Busy bees

Worker bees always have plenty to do in the nest. When a bee returns with pollen and nectar—taken from flowers—the other bees gather around to collect the food. Workers also make the nest cells. They build these cells from wax taken from glands on the underside of the bee's abdomen. The bee pulls out thin flakes of wax and kneads it with her mouthparts until it is soft enough to use for building.

Equipped for work

All the tools needed by a worker bee are on her own body. On each front leg there are long hairs used to brush off pollen that has been collected on the head and front of her body. On the middle legs there are fringes of hair for removing pollen from the forelegs and a spike for taking wax from glands in the abdomen. On each hind leg is a pollen basket—a special area lined with hairs where pollen is carried.

Killer bees

Africanized bees—also known as killer bees—look very similar to honeybees. They are slightly smaller, but only an expert can tell them apart. Unlike honeybees, they are easily annoyed and stay angry for longer. Although their sting is not worse than a honeybee's, they attack in a much larger group, or swarm. A few humans have been killed by their stings. Africanized bees were first brought to America by scientists. These scientists were trying to find ways to make more honey and mated them with wild bees. This new breed of bee escaped into the wild in South America during the 1950s. They are now found in South and Central America, and in the southern United States. The first Africanized bee was found in the United States in 1990 in Texas. They have since spread to California, Florida, and New Mexico.

A worker honeybee has just returned to her colony with her pollen baskets full of golden-yellow pollen. Other workers gather around to help her unload the pollen and pack it into cells.

Wasps

Wasps are more useful than they seem. Their larvae, or grubs, feed on other insects such as caterpillars and aphids, which harm garden and food plants. Adult wasps feed mainly on nectar and the juice of ripe fruit. Many kinds of wasps live alone; others live in large colonies. Wasp colonies do not store food, and the whole colony, except the queen, dies in winter.

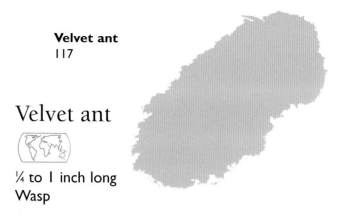

Velvet ant

¼ to 1 inch long
Wasp

Velvet ants are not ants at all but wasps with a thick covering of hair on their bodies. The females search for the nests of bees and other kinds of wasp, then lay their eggs on the larvae. When each velvet ant larva hatches, it eats its host.

Giant hornet

¾ to 1¼ inches long
Wasp

Adult hornets feed on insects and nectar. They live in colonies, in nests built of a papery material that they make by chewing up plants. The nest is usually in a tree or an old building. Larvae feed on insects caught by the adults.

Gall wasp

1/16 to ⅜ inch long
Wasp

These tiny wasps lay their eggs inside the buds of oak trees. The host plant forms a growth, called a gall, around the egg. When the larva hatches it feeds on the gall.

Sawfly

⅛ to ¾ inch long
Wasp relative

Sawflies are related to wasps but do not have the "waist" that wasps have. The female sawfly lays her eggs on willow leaves. Little red galls form on the leaves. When the larvae hatch, they eat the contents of the galls.

Ichneumon wasp

⅛ to 2 inches long
Wasp

Ichneumon wasp
121

The female ichneumon wasp can bore through wood to lay her eggs near the larvae of other insects, such as wood wasps. When the eggs hatch, the ichneumon larvae feed on the host's larvae.

Blue-black spider wasp

Blue-black spider wasp
123

⅜ to 2 inches long
Wasp

The female spider wasp catches spiders to feed her young. She paralyzes the spider with her sting and places it in a nest cell with one of her eggs. When the wasp larva hatches, it eats the spider.

Common wasp

Common wasp
125

⅜ to 1¼ inches long
Wasp

The common wasp is also known as a yellowjacket. The pointed stinger at the end of its abdomen is linked to a bag of poison. The wasp uses its stinger to kill prey and to defend itself.

Paper wasp

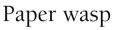

⅜ to 1¼ inches long
Wasp

The paper wasp builds her nest with a papery material that she makes from chewed wood mixed with her spit. She lays her eggs in the cells, and more females join her to help feed the young.

Paper wasp
122

Mud dauber

⅜ to 2 inches long
Wasp

The female mud dauber wasp makes a nest of damp mud. Into each cell she puts an egg and some paralyzed insects for the larva to eat when it hatches.

Mud dauber
124

Sandhills hornet

⅜ to 1¼ inches long
Wasp

These hornets make their papery nests close to the ground in hedges. In hot weather, workers sit at the nest entrance and beat their wings to fan cool air into the nest.

Sandhills hornet
126

Meadow play page

You can find the stickers of insects that live near
flowers on pages 158–159. Stick them on this page
to create your own meadow scene.

Ants and termites

Ants live in huge, well-organized colonies of thousands of individuals. Most colonies make nests with many tunnels in rotting wood or under the ground. Each colony has at least one queen ant, who lays all of the eggs. The workers are also female but they cannot lay eggs. They do all the work of the colony, gathering food and looking after eggs and young. Termites are not related to ants, but they too build large nests with special chambers for eggs, young, and food storage.

Fire ant

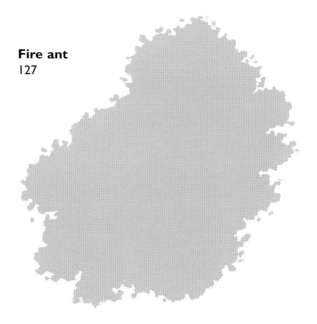

Fire ant
127

¹⁄₁₆ to 1 inch long
Ant

The fire ant has a powerful bite and sting, which are very painful even to humans. It hunts other insects, which it stings to death, but it also eats seeds, fruit, and flowers. It makes nests in the ground or under logs or stones.

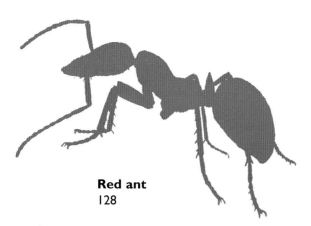

Red ant
128

Red ant

¹⁄₁₆ to 1 inch long
Ant

The main food of red ants is aphid honeydew, a sweet liquid that is made in the stomach of these tiny insects. The ant strokes the aphid to encourage it to release the sugary liquid from its body. Red ants also feed on flower nectar.

Army ant

¹⁄₁₆ to 1 inch long
Ant

Unlike other ants, army ants do not build permanent nests. They march in search of prey, overpowering insects or other small creatures in their way. Every now and then they stop to produce eggs and remain in one place until the young have developed. The worker ants link their bodies, making a temporary nest called a bivouac to protect the queen and young.

Army ant
129

Harvester ant

¹⁄₁₆ to 1 inch long
Ant

These ants get their name from their habit of feeding on seeds and grains. When the ants find a supply of seeds near their nest, they leave scent trails to lead others in their colony to the food. In times of plenty, the ants collect more seeds than they can eat and store them in special areas in the nest.

Harvester ant
130

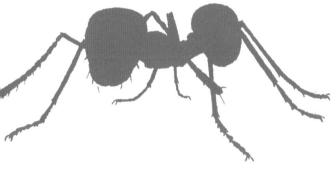

Carpenter ant

¹⁄₁₆ to 1 inch long
Ant

Colonies of carpenter ants make their nests in rotten tree trunks, poles, or wooden buildings. They often cause a great deal of damage. As with all ants, the queen lays all the eggs for the colony. As she lays, worker ants remove the eggs and take them to chambers in the nest where they are cared for.

Carpenter ant
131

Worker termite

Up to ⅜ inch long
Termite

These termites build spectacular mound-shaped nests in savanna areas. The huge mounds can be up to 16 feet tall and are made of soil mixed with the termites' saliva.

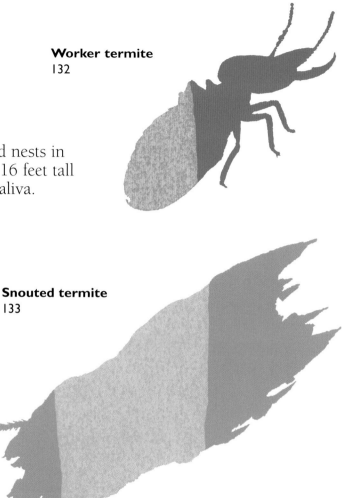

Worker termite
132

Snouted termite

Up to 2¼ inches long
Termite

Most termite colonies have special soldier termites to defend them against enemies such as ants that may attack their nests. These soldier termites have long snouts, through which they spray sticky, bad-smelling fluid at ants and other enemies.

Snouted termite
133

Subterranean termite
134

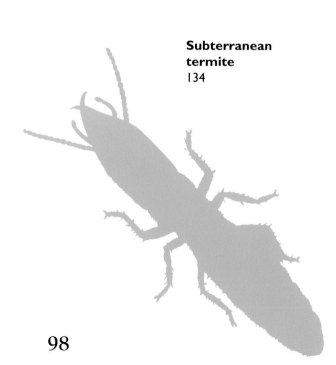

Subterranean termite

¼ to ⅜ inch long
Termite

These termites build underground nests. They live in warm, wooded areas, and eat the wood of rotting trees and roots. Unlike ant larvae, which have to be looked after by worker ants, termite larvae are independent and active as soon as they hatch.

Drywood termite

Up to 1 inch long
Termite

These termites attack the wood of buildings, furniture, and even stored timber. Special tiny organisms in their gut help them digest this tough food. The soldier termites have larger heads and jaws than the others, and their job is to defend the colony against enemies.

Drywood termite
135

Leaf-cutter ant
136

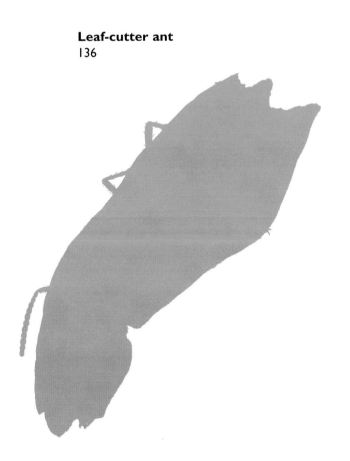

Leaf-cutter ant

¹⁄₁₆ to 1 inch long
Ant

These ants grow their own food. They bite off pieces of leaves with their strong scissorlike jaws and carry them back to their underground nest. Here the leaves are chewed up and mixed with droppings to make compost heaps. The ants eat the special fungus that grows on this compost.

Spiders, scorpions, slugs, and snails

Few small creatures arouse such fear in people as spiders, yet nearly all spiders are completely harmless to humans. Only a few, such as the funnel-web spider, have a venomous bite that is dangerous to people. In fact, spiders do humans a service by keeping the insect population under control. Spiders and their relatives, such as scorpions and mites, are arachnids, not insects. They have four pairs of legs and do not have wings or antennae. Scorpions, too, have a fearsome reputation, and some do have stings that can be fatal to humans.

Other invertebrates (animals without a backbone) include slugs and snails. These make a slimy mucus, which allows them to move more easily.

A yellow mass of baby garden spiders starts to separate and move away along strands of silk when danger threatens.

Armored millipede

101

Hunters

Many carnivorous insects are fierce hunters, seeking out prey and killing them with venomous stings or bites, or slicing them up with razor-sharp jaws.

Thread-waisted wasp with caterpillar prey

Thread-waisted wasp

A female thread-waisted wasp uses its stinger not to kill prey but to paralyze it (prevent it from moving its limbs). She carries it back to her burrow and lays an egg on it. When the grub hatches from the egg, the grub feeds on the fresh meat of the paralyzed prey.

A stinger is a modified egg-laying tube, so only females can sting.

Scorpion

A hunting scorpion comes out at night to look for spiders and insects. The scorpion grabs the prey with a pair of large pincers called pedipalps. If the prey is large or struggling, it uses its sting to paralyze or kill the victim before eating it. The scorpion finds its prey mostly by its sense of touch, using the fine hairs on its body.

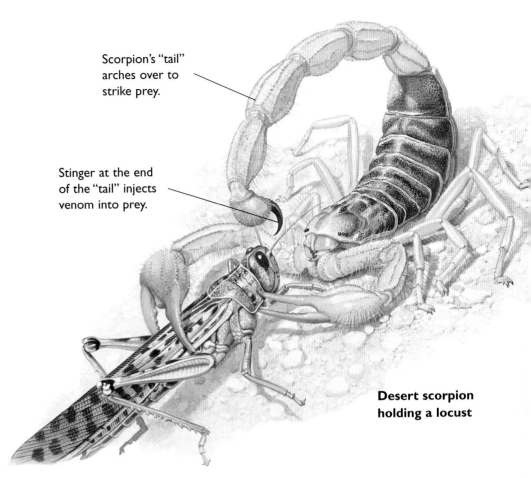

Scorpion's "tail" arches over to strike prey.

Stinger at the end of the "tail" injects venom into prey.

Desert scorpion holding a locust

Mantis and fly

Praying mantis

Powerful jaws and lightning-fast reactions make the praying mantis one of the insect world's deadliest hunters. The mantis stands perfectly still, waiting for unsuspecting prey to come within striking range of its strong forelegs.

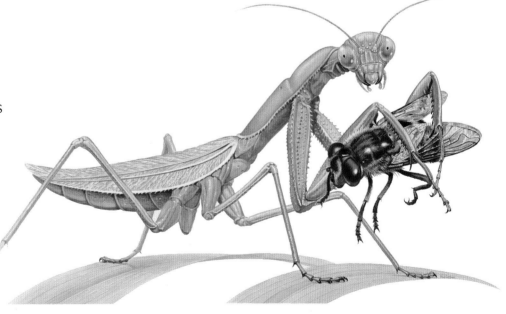

Spiders

All spiders are hunters, feeding mostly on small insects. However, some of the larger species, such as the bird-eating spider, can catch small animals and birds. All spiders can make silk with special glands at the end of their abdomen, but not all build webs. Some spiders use silk to line their burrows, and some make silken traps that they use to snare prey. Young spiders use long strands of silk to help them "fly" away and find new territories.

Crab spider

Crab spider
137

¹⁄₁₆ to ³⁄₈ inch long
Arachnid

This spider moves sideways like a crab. Some crab spiders are dark brown or black, but those that sit on flowers to wait for prey are usually brightly colored to match the petals.

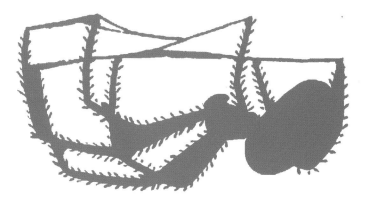

Orchard spider
138

Orchard spider

¹⁄₁₆ to 1¼ inches long
Arachnid

The orchard spider does not make a web. It simply sits on the branch of a tree and grabs any moth that comes near with its strong front legs. It may release a scent that attracts the moths to it.

Water spider
139

Water spider

¹⁄₁₆ to ¾ inch long
Arachnid

This is the only spider that spends its whole life in water. It spins a bell-shaped home of silk, which is attached to water plants. The spider fills it with bubbles of air brought from the surface and sits inside, waiting for prey to come near.

Green lynx spider

⅛ to ⅝ inch long
Arachnid

The lynx spider is a fast-moving, active hunter. It uses its long legs to form a basketlike trap around its prey, which it kills with a venomous bite. Its green color helps keep it hidden when it rests on leaves.

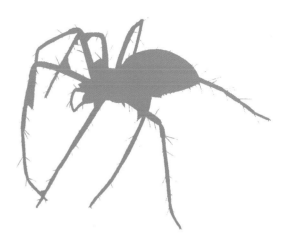

Green lynx spider
140

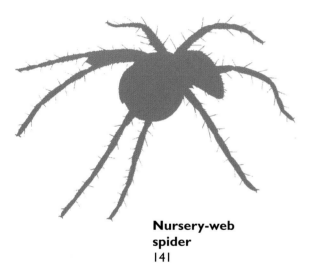

Nursery-web spider
141

Nursery-web spider

¼ to 1 inch long
Arachnid

The nursery-web spider does not build a web to catch prey but to protect her young. She carries her eggs with her until they are almost ready to hatch. Then she spins a web over the eggs to protect them while they hatch. She stands guard nearby.

Black-and-yellow argiope
142

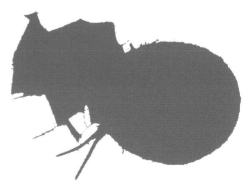

Black-and-yellow argiope

¾ to 1⅛ inches long
Arachnid

The female spider spins a web of sticky silk up to 2 feet across on which to trap her prey. She usually eats the web and rebuilds it each night.

Black widow spider

½ inch long
Arachnid

The female black widow has comblike bristles on her back legs, which she uses to throw strands of silk over prey that gets caught in her web. She has a poisonous bite—her venom is more deadly than rattlesnake venom. Male black widows do not bite.

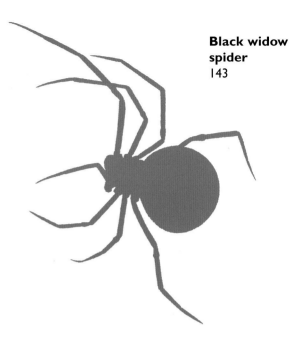

**Black widow
spider**
143

Wolf spider
144

Wolf spider

⅛ to 1½ inches long
Arachnid

Wolf spiders are fast-moving hunters. They creep up on victims and seize them after a final speedy dash. Most do not make webs. Wolf spiders have three sets of eyes that help them to find prey.

Red-kneed tarantula

3½ inches long
Arachnid

Red-kneed tarantula
145

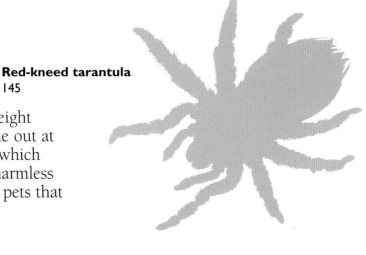

Tarantulas can have legs spanning almost eight inches. Most hide during the day and come out at night to hunt insects and small creatures, which they kill with a venomous bite. They are harmless to people and are becoming so popular as pets that they could soon become rare in the wild.

106

Spitting spider

⅜ inch long
Arachnid

This unusual hunter approaches its victim and spits out two lines of a sticky substance from glands near its mouth. These fall in zigzags over the prey, pinning it down. The spider then kills its prey with a bite.

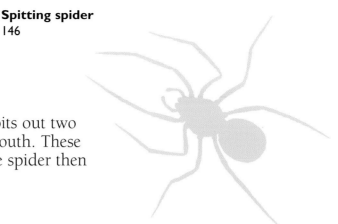

Spitting spider
146

Purse-web spider
147

Purse-web spider

⅜ to 1 inch long
Arachnid

This spider builds a silken tube in a sloping burrow in the ground. The top of the tube extends aboveground and is camouflaged with leaves. When an insect lands on the tube, the spider grabs it through the walls of the tube with her sharp fangs. She then drags it inside.

Trapdoor spider

⅜ to 2 inches long
Arachnid

The burrow of the trapdoor spider has a hinged lid at the top. The spider waits in its burrow until it senses the movement of prey overhead. It then pops out of the door, grabs the prey, and drags it back into its burrow.

Trapdoor spider
148

Cell spider

¾ inch long
Arachnid

These spiders have only six eyes—most spiders have eight. They spend the day hiding under stones and come out at night to hunt wood lice. The cell spider can pierce a wood louse's armor with its huge, sharp fangs.

Cell spider
149

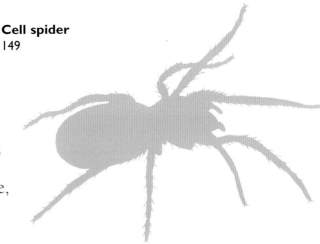

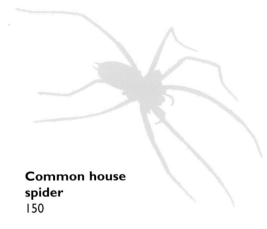

Common house spider
150

Common house spider

¹⁄₁₆ to ¾ inch long
Arachnid

The house spider has long legs covered with strong bristles. It builds its large, flat web in any quiet corner of a house, garage, or shed. It stays by the web, waiting for prey to get tangled in its sticky strands.

Golden silk spider
151

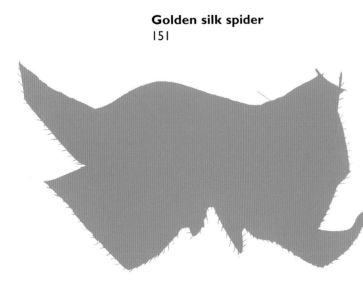

Golden silk spider

¹⁄₁₆ to 1½ inches long
Arachnid

The female golden silk spider is eight or nine times the length of the male and may weigh a hundred times as much. The male's size is an advantage when he tries to get close to the female to mate with her. He is too small for her to bother attacking and he is left alone.

Funnel-web spider

About 1¼ inches long
Arachnid

This spider makes a funnel-shaped web that leads into an underground burrow. If a creature walks across the web, the spider senses the vibrations and rushes out for the kill. Funnel-webs prey on frogs, lizards, and insects. They have a very poisonous bite.

Funnel-web spider
152

Lichen spider
153

Lichen spider

⅜ to 1½ inches long
Arachnid

Mottled colors help keep this spider well hidden on lichen-covered tree bark. Tufts of tiny hairs on its legs break up any shadows that might show predators that it is there. If an enemy is close by, it flattens itself even more against the bark and is very hard to see.

Jumping spider

⅛ to ⅜ inch long
Arachnid

Unlike most spiders, the jumping spider has good eyesight. When it has spotted something, it leaps onto its victim. Before jumping, it attaches a silk thread that it uses as a safety line. It then uses this line to return to its hideout.

Jumping spider
154

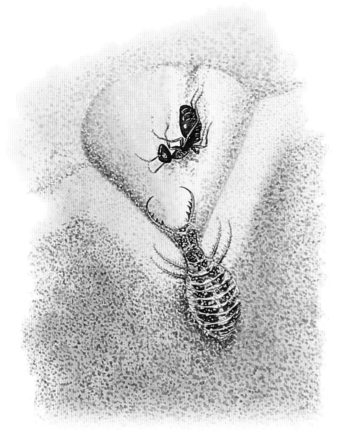

If an ant tumbles down the steep sides of the ant lion's pit, it cannot escape.

Trap setters

Some hunting insects and arachnids go out and search for prey, relying on speed and power to catch their victims. Others use traps, tricks, and lures that allow them to surprise their prey.

Ant lion

The larva of the ant lion is a fierce predator with spiny jaws. It sets a trap for its prey by digging a pit in sandy soil and sitting half-buried in the bottom. It tosses sand at passing ants and insects so that they fall into the pit—and into its jaws.

Assassin bug

Some assassin bugs lure prey with scents they pick up from plants. Victims are injected with saliva. The saliva kills the prey and turns the victim's insides into liquid, which the insect then drinks. Assassin bugs sometimes steal prey caught in spiders' webs.

Assassin bug stabs prey with its feeding tube.

The door has a hinge made of silk threads.

Trapdoor spider

The trapdoor spider ambushes its victims. Its burrow has a hinged door at the top. The spider waits inside until it senses the movement of prey overhead. Suddenly it flips up the door, grabs the prey, and pulls it down into the burrow.

The spider uses special spines on its jaws to dig the burrow.

The spider holds the "net" with its four front legs.

Ogre-faced spider

This spider hangs from a network of dry silk threads. It holds a rectangular, sticky web, which it uses as a net to catch prey. When prey comes near, the spider stretches out the web and throws it over the passing insect. It bundles up its catch and takes it away to eat.

Scorpions and other arachnids

There are about 1,500 kinds of scorpions living in warm parts of the world, from deserts to rain forests. A few kinds of scorpions have venom strong enough to kill a human. The tiny mites and ticks are related to scorpions. Mites eat aphid eggs and prey on other small insects. Some also live as parasites on other animals. Ticks feed on the blood of birds, mammals, and reptiles.

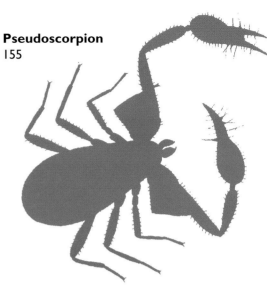

Velvet mite

Up to ³/₁₆ inch long
Mite

This mite gets its name from the thick, soft hair that covers its rounded body. Adult velvet mites lay their eggs on the ground. When the larvae hatch, they live as parasites on insects and spiders, feeding on their body fluids.

Velvet mite
156

Pseudoscorpion

⅝ to 1¾ inches long
False scorpion

These tiny, soil-dwelling relatives of the scorpion have no stingers. Instead, they have venom glands in their pedipalps—the"feelers" that they use when attacking prey. Pseudoscorpions spin silk cocoons in which to spend the winter.

House dust mite

¹/₁₀₀ to ²/₁₀₀ inch long
Mite

These mites are common in houses throughout the world. They feed on scales of human skin found in house dust. Their droppings contain materials that can cause allergies or asthma (difficulty in breathing) in some people.

House dust mite
157

112

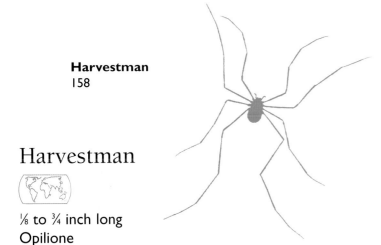

Harvestman
158

Harvestman

⅛ to ¾ inch long
Opilione

Also known as the daddy longlegs, this relative of spiders has a rounded body, without the narrow waist typical of spiders. The harvestman hunts insects, usually at night.

Scorpion

⅛ to ¾ inch long
Scorpion

2 to 2¾ inches long
Scorpion

The scorpion finds prey mostly by its sense of touch, using fine hairs on its body. It grabs the prey in its huge claws and then swings its stinger forward over its body to inject poison into the creature. This paralyzes or kills the victim.

Tick

1/16 to ⅛ inch long
Parasitic arachnid

Ticks are parasites—they live by feeding on the blood of birds, mammals, and reptiles. They stay on the host for several days while feeding, attached by their strong mouthparts. Some species may pass on diseases as they feed.

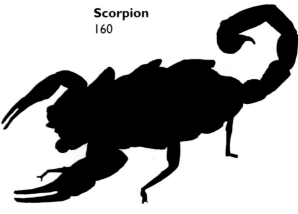

Tick
159

Scorpion
160

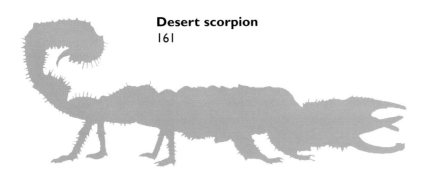

Desert scorpion
161

Desert scorpion

Up to 5½ inches long
Scorpion

This scorpion lives in the southwestern United States. It is very venomous and preys mostly on small insects. Its sting is painful to humans, but not lethal.

Desert play page

You can find the stickers of insects that live in hot climates on pages 159–160. Stick them on this page to create your own desert scene.

Young arachnids and insects

Young insects and arachnids are tiny and in danger of being eaten by prey. Few species look after their newborn young, so their young usually have to look out for themselves. Many die soon after birth.

Spittlebug nymph

A spittlebug is a soft-bodied, plant-eating insect. Its nymph (baby) produces a bubbly substance that keeps its body from drying out and protects it from parasites and predators.

Spittlebug nymph

Frothy mass hides nymph from predators.

Female centruroides scorpion with young

Centruroides scorpion

Scorpions do not lay eggs but give birth to living young. Female centruroides scorpions fold one or more pairs of legs under them to form a "birth basket" that catches the young as they are born. The newborn scorpions climb up her legs and onto her back. She carries them around like this for a few weeks while they grow.

Common earwig

The female common earwig lays her eggs in a burrow and stays close to protect them. She often licks them to keep them clean. If the eggs become scattered, she will collect them together and put them back in the nest. Unusually for an insect, she looks after her young, feeding them until they are big enough to fend for themselves.

Female common earwig with eggs and young

The young scorpions are whitish in color.

The female turns the eggs frequently and cleans them.

Spiderlings

Female spiders create egg sacs to hold their eggs. Some females leave the sacs, while others, such as trapdoor spiders, guard them until the spiderlings (baby spiders) hatch. Others, such as wolf spiders, carry the egg sac around with them. The eggs hatch inside the sac and the spiderlings use a special egg tooth to help them break out of the egg sac when they are born.

Slugs, snails, and other invertebrates

There are many kinds of invertebrate creatures—animals without backbones—throughout the world. These include slugs, snails, worms, millipedes, and centipedes. Slugs and snails are closely related. Both make slime to keep their bodies from drying out and to help them move more easily. Millipedes and centipedes live everywhere, from tropical rain forests to tundra. They are not insects—they have many more legs and do not have wings.

Earthworm
162

Great black slug

6 inches long
Slug

The slug leaves trails of slime wherever it goes and these help it find its way. It feeds mostly on living plants and on rotting plants and animals, which it finds by smell.

Great black slug
163

Earthworm

Up to 11¾ inches long
Megadrile

Earthworms are common in soil all over the world. They come to the surface only at night or in wet weather. Dead plant material is their main food, but they also eat soil, digesting what they can and getting rid of the rest.

Wood louse

⅜ inch long
Crustacean

Wood louse
164

The wood louse is a crustacean and is related to crabs and shrimp. It hides in moist, dark places during the day. It comes out at night to feed on decaying plants and tiny dead creatures.

Centipede

Up to 1¼ inches long
Myriapoda

The centipede moves fast on its 15 pairs of legs. It preys on insects, spiders, and other small creatures. It seizes prey in its sharp claws, which can inject a powerful poison to paralyze the victim.

Centipede
165

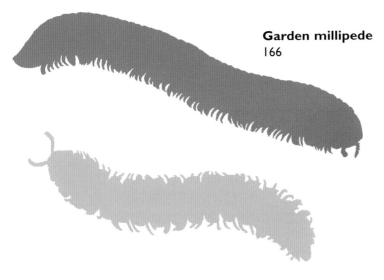

Garden millipede
166

Armored millipede
167

Garden millipede

Up to 3¾ inches long
Myriapoda

"Millipede" means "thousand-footed," but these long-bodied creatures rarely have a thousand legs—most have only a couple of hundred. They are slow-moving plant-eaters that live under stones or tree bark, or hidden in rotting vegetation.

Armored millipede

5 inches long
Myriapoda

Armored millipedes have a hard outer shell. They live in forests, where they feed on leaves and other rotting plants on the forest floor. They have poison glands and some can spray poison to defend themselves against enemies.

Garden snail

3½ inches long
Snail

Garden snail
168

Different types of snails live all over the world. Most snails spend the day inside their shell and come out at night to find food. They move along by making rippling movements of their fleshy "foot." They produce a layer of slime, which they slide along on.

119

Creatures that glow

Some creatures have developed the amazing ability to glow in the dark. Chemical reactions inside their bodies produce light, which the insects use to attract mates, lure prey, or scare off attackers.

Fungus gnat larva

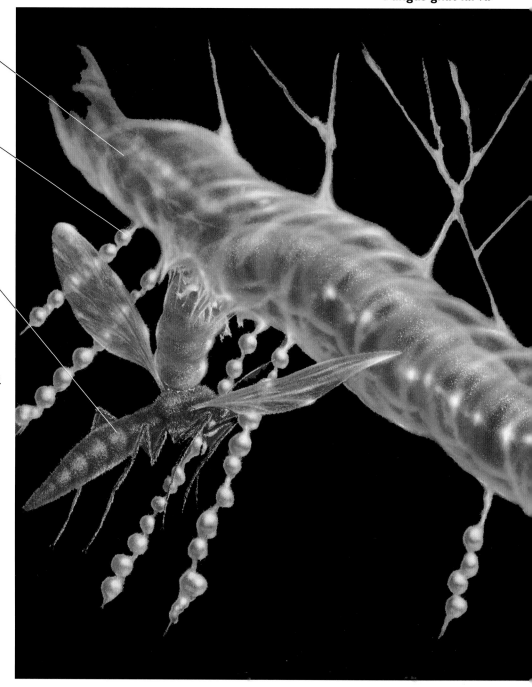

The nest is a tube of silk attached to the cave roof.

Up to 70 silky threads, covered in sticky droplets, hang from the nest.

As well as prey, adult fungus gnats may also get stuck on the threads, but they usually manage to escape.

Fungus gnat

The fungus gnat is a flylike insect. Lying in a tubular nest that hangs from a cave ceiling, a fungus gnat larva makes the tip of its abdomen glow. This lures its prey such as midges and moths. The insects fly toward the light and become trapped on the sticky threads that dangle from the nest.

120

Railroad beetle

The adult female or larva of the railroad beetle looks similar to a worm. If threatened while hunting at night, it scares away its attacker by suddenly switching on its glowing body lights. These look like the windows of a night train.

Head glows a bright red and its body a pale, greenish yellow.

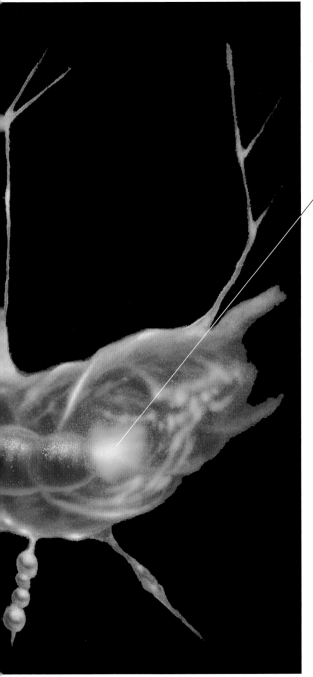

Larva shines its light onto the threads to make them glitter.

Female firefly

A female firefly is wingless. At dusk, she crawls up a grass stem and waves her glowing abdomen in the air to attract a male flying by. Some fireflies use their lights in self-defense, flashing them to warn predators that they taste unpleasant.

Yellowish-green light is produced on the underside of the abdomen.

Female firefly

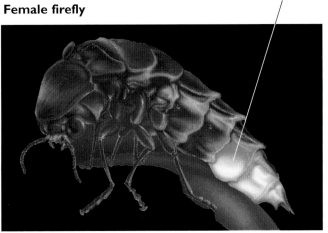

Glossary

abdomen The third and hindmost part of an insect's body, below its waist.

antenna (Plural: antennae) One of a pair of "feelers" on the head—long, jointed organs that can sense things by touch, smell, or even hearing.

arachnid An arthropod with a hard external (outer) skeleton, two body sections, eight legs, and fanglike pincers. Arachnids include spiders, scorpions, ticks, and mites.

arthropod Any of a large group of animals with a hard outer skeleton and jointed body parts. The arthropods consist of insects, crustaceans, and arachnids.

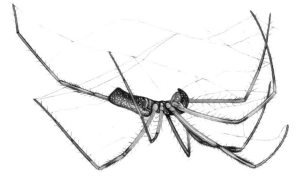

cell A six-sided compartment in the nest of a bee or wasp, often used to store food or eggs.

chrysalis The pupa of a butterfly.

cocoon A silken case that protects some pupae.

cold-blooded Describes an animal that cannot keep its blood at a steady temperature except by seeking out warm or cool places. Insects and other invertebrates are cold-blooded.

colony A large group of insects that live together, usually in a nest. Ants, termites, and some wasps and bees lives in colonies.

crustacean Any of various small animals having a hard external (outer) skeleton, five to seven pairs of legs, and two pairs of antennae. Examples are barnacles, lobsters, and crabs.

fangs Pointed mouthparts, sometimes used to inject venom into prey.

gland A part of the body that produces special substances, such as poisons, which are passed to the outside of the body or into the blood. A gland in a scorpion, for example, makes the venom for its stinger.

halteres The hind wings of a fly, which are reduced to a pair of small, knobbly structures. Halteres help the fly to maintain balance during flight.

host An animal on or in which a parasite, such as a flea, lives and feeds.

insect An invertebrate that has a hard outer skeleton, a body divided into three parts, six legs, a pair of antennae, and wings.

invertebrate An animal that does not have a spine, such as an insect, slug, or beetle.

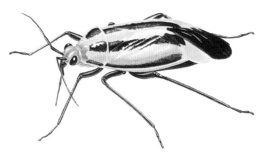

larva (Plural: larvae) A young insect that looks completely different from its adult form.

metamorphosis The dramatic change in body shape as a young animal becomes an adult, such as when a caterpillar becomes a butterfly.

myriapod Any of several kinds of small animals having bodies consisting of many segments and having at least nine pairs of legs. They include the centipedes and millipedes.

nectar A sugary liquid made by plants that attracts insects. While an insect is feeding on nectar, it picks up pollen that it may then take on to the next flower. If pollen reaches the female part of the plant, then that plant is fertilized and can produce seeds.

nymph In insects that do not have a pupa stage in their development, the nymph is the young, wingless form that emerges from the egg.

ovipositor A long organ for laying eggs. It may be specially shaped for laying eggs in wood or in the bodies of other creatures.

parasite A creature that lives on or inside the body of another animal, getting nourishment from it but giving nothing in return. Head lice and fleas are parasites that live on human beings.

pollen Tiny grains made by the male parts of a flower. Pollen must reach the female parts of another flower so that seeds can form.

predator An animal that hunts and eats some other kind of animal, called its prey.

prey An animal that is hunted and eaten by some other animal, called a predator.

proboscis Mouthparts specially adapted for sucking food such as nectar from flowers.

pupa (Plural: pupae) In insects that change their form completely as they develop, the pupa is the stage at which the young insect turns into the adult. It stops moving and feeding and may surround itself with a protective cocoon.

scavenger An animal that lives by eating dead meat.

species One type of animal.

spinnerets The fine, jointed tubes at the end of a spider's abdomen. Silk for spinning a web comes out of a spider's body through the spinnerets.

thorax The second part of an insect's or arachnid's body, between the head and the abdomen. An insect's legs are attached to the thorax.

venom A liquid made by an insect or arachnid that is used to kill or paralyze prey.

vertebrate Animal with a backbone—fish, mammals, reptiles, amphibians, and birds are all vertebrates.

List of creatures

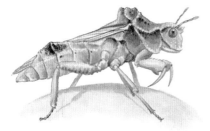

A

ambush bug 23
American cockroach 41
Angola mantis 56
ant
    army 97
    carpenter 97
    fire 96
    harvester 97
    leaf-cutter 99
    red 96
aphid 22
armored millipede 119
army ant 97
assassin bug 24
atlas moth 77

B

backswimmer 28
bark louse 25
bedbug 23
bees 88–89
beetle
    carrion 34
    click 35
    Colorado 35
    darkling 35
    jewel 34
    longhorn 34
    rhinoceros 35
    violin 35
biddy 62
biting midge 69
black fly 71
black widow spider 106
black-and-yellow argiope 105
blowfly 70
blue-black spider wasp 93
boll weevil 34
bumblebee 88
bush katydid 48
butterflies 80–81

C

cabbage white butterfly 81
Cairns birdwing butterfly 80
Carolina locust 51

carpenter ant 97
carpenter bee 89
carrion beetle 34
cat flea 25
cell spider 108
centipede 119
chigoe flea 24
cicada 22
click beetle 35
clothes moth 76
clubtail dragonfly 63
cockroaches 40–41
Colorado beetle 35
common earwig 44
common house spider 108
common scorpionfly 62
common stone fly 57
common wasp 93
copper butterfly 81
cotton boll moth 77
crab spider 104
crane fly 69
cuckoo bee 89

D

damselfly 62
dance fly 71
darkling beetle 35
darter 63
deerfly 71
desert locust 51
desert scorpion 113
diving beetle 33
drywood termite 99

E

earthworm 118
emperor dragonfly 63

F

false stick insect 49
feather louse 25
fire ant 96
firebrat 44
firefly 33
flies 68–71
flower mantis 56
fluminense swallowtail
    butterfly 80

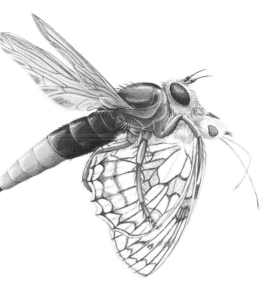

fruit fly 70
funnel-web spider 109

G

gall wasp 92
garden millipede 119
garden snail 119
geometrid moth 76
German cockroach 40
giant hornet 92
giant water bug 29
golden silk spider 108
goliath beetle 32
great black slug 118

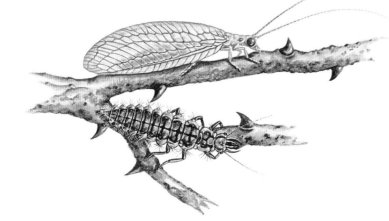

green lacewing 57
green lynx spider 105

H

harlequin cockroach 41
harvester ant 97
harvestman 113
head louse 23
horsefly 68
house dust mite 112
housefly 70
hover fly 69

human flea 25
hummingbird moth 76

I

ichneumon wasp 93

J

jewel beetle 34
jumping spider 109

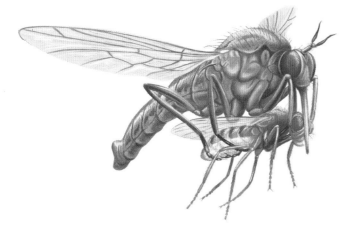

K

katydid 50

L

ladybug 33
large caddis fly 77
leaf-cutter ant 99
leaf-cutter bee 88
leaf insect 49
lichen spider 109
locust 49
longhorn beetle 34
long-horned earwig 45
long-horned grasshopper
    48
luna moth 77

M

Madagascan hissing
    cockroach 40
mantisfly 57
mining bee 89
mole cricket 50

monarch butterfly 81
morpho butterfly 80
moths 76–77
mud dauber 93

N

narrow-winged damselfly 63
nonbiting midge 68
nursery-web spider 105

O

orchard spider 104
orchid bee 88
oriental cockroach 41

P

paper wasp 93
plant bug 23
plasterer bee 88
pseudoscorpion 112
purse-web
    spider 107

Q

Queen Alexandra's
    birdwing butterfly 81

R

red ant 96
red-kneed
    tarantula 106
rhinoceros beetle 35
robber fly 68
rove beetle 32

S

sandhills hornet 93
sawfly 92
scarab beetle 33
scorpion 113
short-horned
    grasshopper 48
silverfish 45
skimmer 63
snakefly 56
snouted termite 98

spider
  black widow 106
  black-and-yellow
    argiope 105
  cell 108
  common house 108
  crab 104
  funnel-web 109
  golden silk 108
  green lynx 105
  jumping 109
  lichen 109
  nursery-web 105
  orchard 104
  purse-web 107
  red-kneed tarantula 106
  spitting 107
  trapdoor 107
  water 104
  wolf 106
spitting spider 107
spittlebug 24
spur-throated
  grasshopper 51
stick insect 51
stingless bee 89
stinkbug 22
striped earwig 45
subterranean termite 98
swallowtail butterfly 80

T

termites 96–99
tick 113
tiger beetle 32
tiger moth 77
trapdoor spider 107

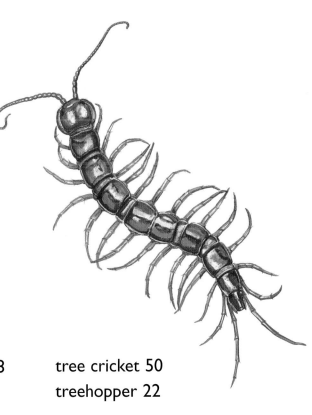

tree cricket 50
treehopper 22

V

velvet ant 92
velvet mite 112
violin beetle 35

W

wasps 92–93
water boatman 29
water bugs 28–29
water measurer 29
water scorpion 28
water spider 104
water stick insect 28
whirligig beetle 32
wolf spider 106
wood louse 118
worker termite 98

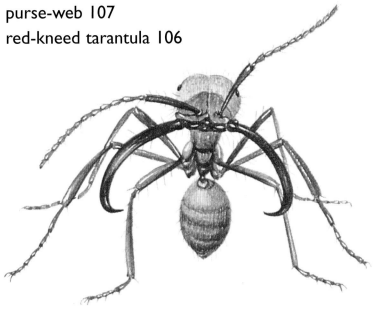

Acknowledgments

ARTWORK CREDITS

Insects, spiders, and other invertebrates
Robin Boutell, Richard Coombs, Joanne Cowne,
Sandra Doyle, Bridget James, Anne Jennings,
Elizabeth Kay, Steve Kirk, Adrian Lascom,
Alan Male, Colin Newman, Obin, Steve Roberts,
Bernard Robinson, Eric Robson, Peter Sarson,
Roger Stewart, Michael Woods, Colin Woolf

Habitat Symbols
Roy Flookes

PHOTOGRAPHIC CREDITS
8–9 P.K. Sharpe/Oxford Scientific Films;
11 Sinclair Stammers/Science Photo Library;
14–15 Stephen Dalton/Oxford Scientific Films;
19 Claude Nuridsany & Marie Perennon/Science Photo Library;
27 Adrian Warren/Ardea; **30–31** Paul A. Souders/CORBIS;
37 Stephen Dalton/NHPA; **46–47** Mark Bolton/CORBIS;
53 Claude Nuridsany & Marie Perennon/Science Photo Library;
60–61 Kevin R. Morris/CORBIS;
64 Harold Taylor/Oxford Scientific Films;
65 Ken Preston-Mafham/Premaphotos Wildlife;
79 Bob Fredrick/Oxford Scientific Films;
91 David Thompson/Oxford Scientific Films;
117 Claude Nuridsany & Marie Perennon/Science Photo Library